Dear Romance Reader,

Welcome to a world of breathtaking passion and never-ending romance.
Welcome to *Precious Gem Romances*.

It is our pleasure to present *Precious Gem Romances*, a wonderful new line of romance books by some of America's best-loved authors. Let these thrilling historical and contemporary romances sweep you away to far-off times and places in stories that will dazzle your senses and melt your heart.

Sparkling with joy, laughter, and love, each *Precious Gem Romance* glows with all the passion and excitement you expect from the very best in romance. Offered at a great affordable price, these books are an irresistible value—and an essential addition to your romance collection. Tender love stories you will want to read again and again, *Precious Gem Romances* are books you will treasure forever.

Look for eight fabulous new *Precious Gem Romances* each month—available only at Wal★Mart.

Lynn Brown, Publisher

www.1stChoiceUsedBooks.com

www.1stChoiceUsedBooks.com

ANNIE'S RAINBOW

Jean Clark

Zebra Books
Kensington Publishing Corp.

http://www.zebrabooks.com

*To my husband, Paul, who encouraged me to follow
my dream. Thanks to my teachers, my critique and
plotting groups, and members of the online Romance
Writers List and Clues-N-News. Special thanks to
my mentor, Sandra Paul. I appreciate you all.*

ZEBRA BOOKS are published by

Kensington Publishing Corp.
850 Third Avenue
New York, NY 10022

Copyright © 1997 by Barbara Clark

All rights reserved. No part of this book may be reproduced
in any form or by any means without the prior written consent
of the Publisher, excepting brief quotes used in reviews.

If you purchased this book without a cover you should be aware
that this book is stolen property. It was reported as ''unsold
and destroyed'' to the Publisher and neither the Author nor the
Publisher has received any payment for this ''stripped book.''

Zebra and the Z logo Reg. U.S. Pat. & TM Off.

First Printing: December, 1997

Printed in the United States of America
10 9 8 7 6 5 4 3 2 1

Chapter One

Annie Reed jammed on the brakes with a muttered, "Damn." Ahead, a wall of heaving, hairy, reddish brown cattle blocked the graveled road winding through Arizona rangeland.

"Walking steaks," she groaned. As a professionally trained chef, she could name at least a dozen ways to prepare them, but she had no idea how to move the obstinate beasts.

Tapping the steering wheel, Annie studied the problem. She'd survived California earthquakes, fires, floods, and a bad-tempered head chef. Of all the challenges she'd faced, this one was enough to curdle her créme brulée.

One cow—close enough for Annie to see the individual russet hairs on its coat—stared at her, a clump of grass mixed with slobber hanging from both sides of its mouth. The others surrounded her car as they grazed under a peaceful blue sky.

She glanced at her wristwatch. Swallowing the sharp taste of panic, she realized her interview started in fifteen minutes. Her whole career might depend on this job.

Another cow ambled through the clusters of olive green brush. It crossed the road in front of her and stopped, its tail gently swishing against one headlight. Munching a mouthful of leaves and stems, it looked at her, brown eyes wide and wary in its dusty white face.

"Get away!" Annie shouted through her open window.

It answered her with a muffled snort.

Determined to get past the animals, she slipped out the door into the sage-scented desert air. High heels wobbling on the pebbled road, she hesitated. Without the steel of the car between her and the cattle, she felt vulnerable. Even the daintiest animal in the herd weighed a quarter ton. What if one charged? Could she jump into the car in time to escape? She frowned, knowing she had to risk it.

Straightening, she took a breath and flapped her hands. "Shoo. Shoo. Move!"

One looked at her. The others buried their mouths in the thick grass and wild mustard plants.

Squinting in the late-morning sun, Annie waved her arms and tried again. "Go home! Before I turn you into hamburgers."

At that, one cow folded its legs, settled on the sun-warmed gravel, and stared into space. Great jaws moved rhythmically as it chewed.

Disgusted, Annie climbed back into the car and hit the horn. With a startled bawl, the resting cow lurched to its feet and joined the other members of the herd thundering around her little two-door and up the road in a choking cloud of dust.

"Good." She waited for them to clear the road. Another minute passed. Instead of heading out, they gradually slowed and stopped.

"No!" She thumped the steering wheel in exasperation. "You're still in my way."

Frustrated, she sounded the horn again, starting another mad scramble.

Out of nowhere, a cowboy dashed past on a black horse. Bent forward, his muscles straining against his denim shirt, he urged his mount closer to the cattle. The rider raced alongside the stampeding herd, reached the lead animal, and turned the whole rowdy bunch toward an opening in the fence parallel to the road.

After closing the gate behind the last straggler, the broad-shouldered man, his mouth set in a straight line, kicked his horse into a trot toward her. His brown, wide-brimmed hat shaded the rest of his features, but from the rigid set of his shoulders, she sensed his anger.

Annie tensed.

Searching for a way to defuse the situation, she forced a bright smile and leaned out the window. "That was brilliant. Thanks for moving them."

He faced her, his horse standing at alert. "You're a damned idiot. Want to start a stampede?" His voice was low and angry.

"But—"

"Cattle can get hurt when they're spooked. Break a leg, fall, and be trampled." He closed one hand into a fist. "Or did you even consider that?"

"Sorry, no. They're so big I thought that I might be the one who got hurt."

While she struggled to keep her temper, she couldn't help but admire his long, muscled legs in work-worn jeans and old leather chaps. A lifetime of hard physical work showed in his broad shoulders underneath his denim work shirt, streaked by dust and sweat.

His horse minced a few steps sideways. The cowboy patted its glossy neck, then took off his hat, still scowling at her, and raked long fingers through his auburn hair. Fierce desert sunlight revealed dark brown eyebrows winged across green eyes, a slight bump in his proud nose, and a firm mouth.

"City girl," he said curtly.

Stung by his attitude, she demanded, "Who are you? I said I was sorry. You don't own the road."

"Yes, I do. And you damn near ran into my cows. You're on my property. Those're my cattle."

"Well, I didn't know. The road's not marked and the gate was already open."

"One of Russell's dudes probably left it open taking a short-cut to town."

Annie cleared her throat, fighting her anger and frustration. "If you'll tell me how to get to Sunrise Peaks Ranch, I'll get off your land."

"I should have known you were headed to Ben Russell's," he stated in a cold voice. "More your type of place than a real cattle ranch."

Annie glared at him. "I hope so. He's expecting me."

"Another dude?" Settling the hat on his head, he crossed one powerful hand over the other, reins held slack, and bent forward as if to see her better through the open window.

She shivered under the sudden impact of his hard gaze. "That's my business. Just give me the directions, please, and I'll leave."

He studied her a moment longer. "Take the left fork past the stand of ocotillos."

"Ocotillos? And they are . . . ?"

"Probably look like cactus to you. They're tall, thorny canes with small leaves and red flowers."

"Thanks, Mr.—?"

He slashed his hand down, ignoring her effort to learn his name. "Don't honk your damned horn around my cattle again."

He whirled and rode away.

"Welcome to friendly Arizona," Annie muttered.

Two riders topped the crest of the ridge to her left. Seeing them reminded her of the commanding way the cowboy had sat astride his big black horse. Even the flash of his green eyes, angry and contemptuous, had left their impression.

She felt a stab of remorse. The cattle were his livelihood. What if she had injured one?

Maneuvering her car to avoid fist-sized rocks in the rutted road, she thought about her reaction to him. She didn't want to admit, even to herself, that he'd shaken her.

"Snap out of it," she told herself as she slowed to avoid a jackrabbit. "This job interview is more important than some touchy cowboy's snap judgment."

Ten minutes later she faced another cowboy—her prospective employer—across a cluttered desk. Unlike the first, this man's shirt wasn't covered with dust, but nicely pressed and heavily embroidered in a flamboyant western motif. Dressed in dark slacks, the burly rancher exuded heavy-handed authority behind his smile. She met that smile with one of her own. "I'm Annie Reed, here for the job you offered me."

"Job? That's not settled yet." The flare of interest in his eyes when she'd first walked into his office cooled.

Annie's palms grew damp. Willing her voice to sound calm, she said, "Mr. Russell, on the phone you said to come in for the position of chef."

"Now, don't get yourself all riled up." Tipping back in his leather chair, he read her short resumé.

It was quiet in the knotty-pine paneled office. Annie hid her inner turmoil and listened to the sounds outside; conversation, laughter, the faint *clop, clop* of passing horses.

Finished, he set the paper down and smiled patronizingly. "Well, little lady, that's mighty thin readin'."

With an abrupt motion, he leaned forward and dropped the papers on the desk, his smile gone. "Impress me. Sunrise Peaks has an international reputation to uphold."

Annie straightened, trying to hide her desperation. Never let them see you sweat, she thought, and put on an air of confidence. "Well, for starters I'm a graduate of the Cooking Institute of America in St. Helena, California."

"What else?"

She took a breath. "I worked as a pastry and dessert chef's assistant for several months while I attended classes."

"Why isn't his name listed as a reference?"

Annie remembered Chef Franco's fury when he discovered she'd saved surplus rolls, cookies, and pastries, passing them on to people in the residential motel where she lived. She'd had the restaurant owner's permission. In spite of that, Franco had fired her.

"I didn't want to bother him." Her honesty made her add, "We had an argument."

Russell tossed her resumé across the desk. "Making desserts hardly qualifies you as a gourmet chef for our sophisticated clients."

"I'm a graduate of the Cooking Institute," she repeated. "I'm able to prepare a wide variety of cuisine." She folded one hand over the other to hide her trembling. "Before that, I had the experience they required to enroll. The registrar accepted my year as cook and bread maker at the Daily Bread restaurant. Altogether, I'm well qualified."

"Not for here. Start your own guest ranch if that's what turns you on."

Her breath caught in her throat, but she forced a question through frozen lips. "You mean I don't have the job?"

He stood and moved around the desk to her, a slow smile spreading across his handsome features. "Sorry, gal, you're an attractive little filly, but I can't hire you for the chef's position."

He propped his hip against one corner of the desk. "Still, you're a bright lady. You'd fit in real well here in another way. Want to be my *personal* assistant? Good money in it, plus lots of entertainment and a suite of rooms in my wing." He reached out a broad, manicured finger to touch her cheek. "I'll treat you real nice. How about it?"

"No, thank you." Stiffly, she pushed her chair backward, rose to her feet, and reached for her resumé. Loathing welled up like bile and burned her stomach. She couldn't stand to be near Russell.

He blocked her, his expression growing hard. "Think about my offer. Jobs are hard to find."

She met his gaze, trying to be cool and icy. "No."

With a shrug, he went back to his computer.

Annie grabbed her papers and marched out of his office.

Back in the small town an hour later, seated in the Coffee Cup Cafe, Annie settled deeper into the orange vinyl booth. The odors of onions, burgers and fries, pine-scented cleanser, and the cook's lethal coffee filled the room. Here she sat in Dripping Springs, Arizona, a nine-hour drive from home, broke, her credit cards maxed out, a hole in the toe of her pantyhose, and drinking the thick sludge this greasy spoon passed off as coffee.

She took a mouthful and tried not to spit it out. Some fly-bitten cow would probably give half a hoof and one ear to use the stuff as insect repellent.

The familiar bustle of the small cafe brought back high school days when she'd worked in Pete's Place after classes. Annie wondered if the management needed a cook or waitress here.

"Warm-up, dearie?" Coffee splashed into her cup, poured by the cheerful waitress with a name tag pinned to the front of her brown and burnt orange uniform.

"Thanks, Verna." Annie dredged up a smile for the friendly woman.

"Pie with the coffee?" Before Annie could answer, Verna added, "Gus prides himself on his baking. People come from miles around to chow down on apple pie and coffee."

In spite of her brief glimpse of Gus—with his stained apron, hairy arms, and sweating face—Annie's stomach growled from hunger. Still, she shook her head. Coffee was all she could afford. "No, thanks."

The waitress asked in a low voice, "What's the matter? You look awfully sad. Boyfriend walk out on you?"

"Nothing like that." Annie gulped some coffee. "The truth is, I'm just about broke." She looked up into the woman's sympathetic eyes and decided to take a chance. "I don't suppose they're hiring here?"

Regretfully, Verna shook her head. "Sorry." She topped off the thick mug. "Save your money. Drink your coffee and sit as long as you like."

"Just a few more minutes. I have to figure out where I'm staying tonight." Annie had a sudden mental picture of sleeping in her car with a stray coyote or two considering her a potential meal in a can. She stifled the thought. "I came here thinking I had a job as chef at the Sunrise Peaks Guest Ranch."

"Ben Russell's place." Verna made a face. "His daddy owned the Peaks when it was a workin' outfit."

"You know him pretty well?"

"Since he was in diapers."

Toying with her paper napkin, Annie gazed out the window at the peaceful scene and wondered what to do next. People strolled along the plank sidewalks, stopping to talk to friends.

She shifted her attention to the high, tree-clad mountains surrounding three sides of the town. It looked like a beautiful place to live.

Verna stopped beside the table with a bowl of soup and two rolls. "Cappy over there ordered this, then changed his mind, said he wanted chili." She nodded toward an elderly, bearded cowboy sitting at the counter. "Don't want good food goin' to waste. Do me a favor and eat this."

"You sure?" Annie's pride warred with acute hunger pangs.

"Eat." Verna slid a small white saucer holding the rolls and three pats of butter toward her.

Annie thanked her and spooned up the homemade beef and vegetable soup. "It's delicious."

Verna turned at the tinkle of the bell hung over one edge of the door. "Gotta go."

A heavy tread and then a slight movement of the padded back told Annie someone had settled in the booth behind her.

While she watched, Verna poured coffee and gave it to the new occupant. She cut a huge wedge of warm apple pie, added a scoop of vanilla ice cream, and carried it to her customer, saying, "Haven't seen you for a week, Jake. Salty finally learn to make decent pies?"

"Hell, no. Damn near killed us with his cooking." The speaker's voice was deeply masculine and laced with the soft drawl so common to these parts.

Verna made a sympathetic noise. "I knew he weren't no great shucks at cooking. What happened this time?"

"Puked my guts out. Boys, too. Doc Patterson said we had food poisoning."

"You poor fellas."

Annie added her silent sympathy.

She heard the click of the man's fork against a plate. He added, "They would've taken it out of his hide if he hadn't hightailed it outta there."

He paused. Annie heard the soft thud of a mug set down on the formica tabletop. "What they said isn't fit for ladies to hear."

Verna poured him more coffee. "Who's fixin' the food now?"

"Travis or me."

Annie's heart began to pound.

The man heaved a disgusted sigh. "Dammit, the crew's ready to cut and run if I don't find a decent cook."

This was her chance! She blurted, "I'll take the job," then turned and knelt to peer over the seat back.

She saw the top of a well-worn brown Stetson and broad shoulders.

Silence met her offer.

Slowly the stranger swiveled his head, and cool green eyes met hers.

She scowled in disgust. "You."

Chapter Two

Jake eyed the woman leaning over the booth in surprise. He was not pleased to see the city girl who'd scared his cattle. "You?" he drawled in mocking response. "*You* want the job?"

She lifted her chin. "Yes." Ducking out of sight behind the booth, she came around the edge to stand beside the table.

With inbred courtesy, he stood, gesturing to the place opposite him. "Have a seat."

She settled into the booth and looked him square in the eye.

He had to admit he liked what he saw. Sunlight streaming in through the front windows glinted off a cloud of coppery gold curls. A broad turquoise and silver clip on one side struggled to tame them. Her slim, straight nose tilted up slightly at the end.

"Can you cook?"

Her shoulders straightened as she gave him a businesslike smile. "Yes, I'm a professional chef. I have the credentials to prove it."

"Can you cook good plain food? He forked a large bite of pie into his mouth, chewing as he studied her.

"Sure. How does prime rib and onion-roasted potatoes sound?" Sapphire blue eyes dared him. He controlled an impulse to grin.

He saw her fingers tremble as she smoothed her turquoise-colored raw silk skirt. *Stephanie had pampered herself with silk, too*. He pushed away the thought, looked at the soft rise of her breasts against the matching blouse, then quickly averted his gaze.

Devouring another bite, he asked, "Do you bake pies, cakes?"

"I assisted a pastry and dessert chef."

Jake eyed her as he gulped his coffee. "Ranch hands want lots of food and nothing fancy. Can you handle that?"

Her eyes flashed fire. "No problem."

Frowning, he looked her up and down. "Steaks?"

"If I don't have to chase them down on the hoof."

"Nope." He swallowed more coffee. "A working ranch's dangerous for a tenderfoot. Hell, even a top cowhand can be hurt."

"A big city is dangerous, and I've survived."

He studied her through narrowed eyes. "Thought you were headed to Ben Russell's."

"He didn't offer me the job I was expecting." Her cheeks flamed, but she faced him without flinching.

"Stay clear of Russell if you work for me."

"I have no intention of seeing Mr. Ben Russell whether I work for you or not."

Gesturing *no more* when Verna brought the coffee pot, Jake kept his attention focused on the young woman in front of him. "What happened?"

Her body tensed, slim fingers curling around one chipped edge of the table. "We had a difference of opinion."

Probably more to it than that, Jake thought, aware of her uneasiness. If she could fix decent food he needed her at the ranch. One more rotten meal and the whole crew would quit. He had to keep them or lose Rainbow Valley. In spite of that, he didn't want to hire her. She looked too vulnerable for ranch life. Worse, she was too enticing. She'd stir up the men. Hell, she was even stirring him up, and he'd had enough experience with women like her to know better.

He watched her finish the soup Verna had brought from the

next booth. Despite has assurances, she looked like she'd prefer to make fancy dishes more than the plain fare his men wanted.

Trouble was, he needed a cook.

He decided to give her a chance. "You're hired." He finished the last chunk of his pie and wiped his mouth.

She acted dumbstruck. "Don't you want to see my resumé?"

He shook his head. "You're a woman. Any woman's gotta cook better than Salty. Got any objections to a contract? You'll work at least six months."

Her eyes widened. "You don't trust me?"

"How else do I know you'll stick?"

"I'm tougher than I look." She tapped the purse beside her on the table. "And I need a job."

"Good, you won't have a problem signing the agreement."

He caught Verna's attention. "Can you rustle me up two sheets of paper, napkins, anything to write on?"

Verna nodded and disappeared through the kitchen door. In a couple of minutes she returned with two paper placemats proclaiming Paradise Cafe on one side.

"Gus bought a load of paper goods from a going-out-of-business sale in Prescott," she said, handing the placemats and a pen to Jake.

Nodding his thanks, he wrote out the agreement, made a copy, then turned both for Annie to read. "This is all I can offer. Plus room and board."

She looked miserable as she read it, and muttered, "I thought I was worth more than that, but beggars can't be choosers."

Silently he gave her a pen and indicated where she should put her name.

She signed both copies. "Here it is, Mr. Stone, your guarantee. One day you'll learn I keep my word."

"We'll see." He added his signature, handed her one copy, and jammed the other in his pocket. "Rainbow Valley Ranch is too important to take chances with a stranger."

Standing, he tossed several bills and coins on the counter. "On me."

He nodded to Verna, donned his hat, and motioned to his new employee. "Let's go."

She didn't like the abrupt order, he could tell by the rebellious expression on her face. Apparently deciding against arguing, she grabbed her purse and slid to the edge of the booth seat.

He caught Verna's attention, as he checked the name on the contract. "I'm signing Annelise on as cook."

"It's Annie, Annie Reed."

"We'll take Annie's car. Travis'll come for Bandit."

"I got it." Verna put her hand on one hip. "Be good to her or I'll have your ears."

Jake watched Annie blush at the low chuckles and grins from the cowboys in the cafe.

He tugged her to her feet. "Car out front?"

She dug in her heels. "Would you please take your hands off and stop rushing me? How do I know you're not some pervert? I can still tear up the contract."

Male laughter filled the cafe. One voice shouted, "Yep, we come fer the pervert round-up once a week."

Another added, "She's pegged you right, Jake."

Ignoring them, he watched Annie gather her composure. She boldly met his gaze. "Answer my question."

"Pervert? Nope."

He snagged her wrist and propelled her toward the door, trying to discount the swift flood of sexual awareness triggered by the sizzling contact with her smooth, delicate skin. "Don't worry, city girl. You're safe with me."

"I doubt that." She pulled away and marched toward her car, obviously struggling to keep her balance in her high heels on the uneven board sidewalk.

They reached her green Civic, parked in front of Mamie's Boutique next to the coffee shop. She moved ahead to open the passenger-side door. A cool breeze kicked up, plastering her skirt against her nicely shaped legs and bottom. He cursed the surge of heat in his groin, and told himself to forget it.

She faced him, the breeze molding the bright material to her breasts. Just what he needed to see. Jake scowled at her.

"I'll drive." He held out his hand for the keys.

"No." She raised a hand to brush the hair out of her eyes. "It's my car. You navigate. I'll do my own driving."

Seeing the determination in her face, he decided to let her win this one. He piled into the passenger side, wedging his long legs into the narrow space. Time enough to out-stubborn her when she saw the kitchen.

"Which way, Mr. Stone?"

"It's Jake." He nodded toward where the street passed Kendall's Hardware. "Go north. Next to Russell's."

She spun the wheel, and he studied her profile. In the close quarters of this compact car, her faint, delicate scent teased him. It reminded him of the sweet, sensuous touch of a woman's lips; the hot, slick glide of smooth, bare skin against his hard body. Dammit, he was determined not to let mindless hormones rule him.

Cutter Holland, Ben's foreman, swung past them in the Peaks' van, carrying a load of passengers. *Dudes,* Jake thought scornfully. Russell catered to them, especially attractive women. He hadn't been nicknamed Randy Russell in high school for nothing.

"Mr. Stone? Jake?" Annie's voice held the slightly exasperated note of someone who'd asked a question several times.

"Yeah?"

"How many people live on your ranch?"

"A crew of four and me. More at haying and roundup."

"Your wife?"

"Not married." He studied her narrowly. "All the men are single. Stick to your pots and pans. No messing around with my crew. Got it?"

"Excuse me, *Mr.* Stone." He saw her slim fingers tighten on the wheel. Her eyes flashed. "I plan to cook, not flirt. Trust me. Cowboys aren't my cup of tea. Besides, I'm no femme fatale."

He opened his mouth to dispute her, then closed it. Better to keep a distance.

Twenty minutes later, the tires hummed as they crossed the wooden bridge over Gold Creek. The high water level promised a good supply through late summer. A narrow stratum of red clay lay just above the clear, racing liquid. He looked beyond the fence lining the opposite bank. Lush green grass, dotted with clusters of blue lupines, and yellow-flowering brittlebush, rippled in the wind. Away from water, the grass thinned out, showing red soil, occasional boulders, cactus, and scrub brush. In the distance rose the great purplish blue bulk of the Bradshaw Mountains.

Closer, a red sandstone butte towered against the high-desert sky. His home ranch sat on the toe of one spur. *My land.* He felt intense pride. The Stone family had held the spread for over a hundred years. He planned to hang on to it no matter what.

"Are we almost there?" Annie's question snapped him out of his thoughts.

"Go right past that clump of cottonwoods."

"Here?"

"Yeah. We've been running beside Rainbow Valley Ranch for the last couple of minutes. This morning you were on the other road west of here."

She turned the car onto the graded ranch road and stopped for Jake to open the heavy wood and wire barrier. Dirt and rocks crunched under the tires as she drove through. Fastening the gate behind Annie's car, he had a sense of impending disaster. A tenderfoot could get into trouble just nosing around the barn.

He sat back as she slowly bumped across the washboard ripples in the hard-packed dirt road.

The car bottomed out on a nasty stretch, but she kept on going.

"Have to get it graded again," he said, wishing he'd done it before hiring Annie, even if money was tight. Stephanie had bitched at him every time they'd hit a bump.

"That or hire a dentist. You know, 'Fix teeth, will travel.' " She turned to smile at him, amusement dancing in her eyes.

At least she had a sense of humor. He hoped it wouldn't evaporate when she saw the kitchen.

Five minutes later they stopped in front of his sprawling ranch house, shaded by cottonwood and sycamore trees.

Annie stepped out of the car with a peculiar sense of coming home. The faded yellow, two-storey house with its shingle roof and wraparound porch overlooked the valley. Cooking from a kitchen with a view like this would be a delight.

A short distance away, six buildings ranged in groups along the high ground. Barns and corrals sat lower down. Cattle grazed in the valley. Here, only the wind sighing through trees, and the sudden piping of an unseen bird broke the silence.

"It's beautiful and so peaceful," she murmured, reveling in the scent of the fresh, sage-spiced breeze. An unseen presence welcomed her. The spirits of men and women who'd stood here in earlier times and gazed out across the wild land, filled with the same sense of wonder.

Excited, she grabbed her purse and faced Jake. "Let's see what I got myself into."

His grim expression wasn't exactly reassuring, she thought, as he led her across a scraggly patch of grass to the ranch house. The white woodwork needed a coat of paint. Weeds in the flower bed by the porch choked the few hardy rosebushes bravely reaching toward the sun.

"Watch the steps." Jake waited with the screen door open. Annie peered into the dim interior.

"Your quarters first." His strong fingers closed around her wrist, starting a slow heat in her blood. She fought to ignore the sensation as he propelled her past the dark, wood-paneled living room so fast that she only caught a fleeting impression of heavy, well-used furniture, braided rugs, a stone fireplace, and the dusty odor of neglect.

At the top of the narrow, steep staircase, he released her, and she followed dutifully as he turned right.

"End rooms are yours." He opened a door, stepping back for her to go ahead. "This used to be my grandmother's sitting room."

The place had a closed-up stuffiness. Across the room, under one window, sat a treadle sewing machine. Annie went to it, touched the ornate gold lettering on the black metal top, and smiled in delight. A potbellied stove had been placed close enough to warm whoever sewed. An antique rocker and a padded wingback chair alongside a table and lamp completed the furnishings.

"Here's your bedroom." He leaned against the doorframe and folded his arms. "There's a lock on the door."

"Why? Have I got something to worry about?"

Jake reddened and rubbed his chin.

She moved away from him. She was here to cook. Nothing more.

Sunlight picked out the muted colors of a handmade quilt on the carved maple bed. The matching dresser with mirror sat against the inside wall. A large braided rug warmed the oak plank floor.

"I love this room!" she exclaimed.

With a jerk of his head, Jake gestured toward the stairs. "Now the kitchen."

Eagerly, she followed him. Her rooms were so darling, she couldn't wait to see the kitchen. Probably needed to be swept and mopped, but that wouldn't take long.

The first thing Annie saw was a long, oilcloth-covered table, army-sized.

She paused beside it. "Just four guys and yourself? This table is huge."

"For now. During roundup there'll be at least six more."

He pushed another door open and they stepped into the biggest—and the dirtiest—kitchen Annie had ever seen.

"Oh, my God," she whispered. A wave of queasiness welled up in her throat as she smelled the sour stench of tainted food and old coffee.

Past the grimy refrigerator, a six-burner stove stood against one wall, its white enameled surface marked with old drips and stains.

Jake spoke from behind her. "Uses propane. Tank's outside. You'll have to check the gauge."

"Check the gauge," she repeated numbly, looking at dishes and pans jumbled across counters on both sides of the sink. Sunlight filtered through a wide dirty window, and limp curtains hung above the modern stainless steel basin.

"Do you have a dishwasher?" She glanced around the room again, thinking she'd missed seeing it.

"Nope. I run a working ranch, no place or money for extras."

Three years of culinary training for this? Pressure behind her eyes and stinging at the back of her throat signaled unwanted tears. She swallowed to ease the tension and continued her survey.

Beyond the counter, a freezer chest guarded one side of a closed door. A black stove, with a broad metal pipe from its back to the ceiling, squatted on the other side. Its four curved legs dented an inch thick metal pad.

"Tell me it doesn't burn wood," Annie begged.

"Yep, it does. Is that a problem?" Jake's expression held a guarded, waiting look.

"I've never—"

"Wood box." He gave it a kick. "The men'll keep it filled."

"But ... " She looked around the food-spattered mess, recalling the surgically clean kitchens where she'd trained. Should she cry? Why bother? Her sense of the ridiculous struck. Trying to stifle a chuckle, she leaned against the scarred work-table. One look at Jake's startled expression brought laughter closer to the surface. She pointed at the new metal sink jammed between old-fashioned counters. "What happened to the original?"

He took off his hat and brushed back sweat-dampened hair. "Dropped a horseshoe. Cracked the porcelain. It leaked."

"You were washing a horseshoe?" She dissolved into silly laughter—and knew it came from being stressed and overtired—while tears ran down her cheeks.

"Miss Reed? Annie?" Jake's firm grip settled on her shoulder.

Wiping tears with the back of her hand, she grinned at him. "When things can't get any worse, laugh."

He looked around the kitchen. "Needs a little cleanin'."

"More than a little." Examining the cupboards, she pulled out a cauldron-sized pot with unidentifiable bits of food stuck inside. "Here's how you got food poisoning."

"And the reason you're here." With an impatient sound, he set his hands on his lean hips and studied her through narrowed eyes.

"Our deal didn't include the labors of Hercules."

He picked up an enormous can and dropped it on the over-flowing trash basket. "It's not bad. No worse than mucking out a stable."

"It's much worse." She heard the shrill tension in her own voice. "I spent years and every penny I could scrape up to learn gourmet cooking. Not how to muck stables."

"Backing out of our deal, *city girl?*"

Refusing to let him intimidate her, Annie straightened her spine and met him glare for glare. "I'll stay the full six months, *country boy.*"

"We'll see." Opening the door into the mudroom, he paused long enough to say, "I've got chores to do. Call when supper's ready."

Sighing, she started a mental To Do list, and found a clean apron tucked away beneath a pile of grimy dishtowels.

She always thought best when she rolled up her sleeves, she mused as she plugged the sink, filled it with hot water, and squirted in soap. Loading a stack of food-encrusted plates and tableware into the bubbles, she gradually became aware of the silence and isolation of the house.

Now, all alone, her defenses crumbled. Hot-tears slid down her cheeks. She scrubbed dried food from a plate thinking that this was her first real job since graduating from the Institute.

"Professional chef," she said in bitter disappointment. All those years of study. Years of dreaming about the salary her position would ultimately bring, and the joy of creating wonderful, unique dishes. She could easily pay off her credit cards, student loans, and car, and put money in the bank. She'd never have to scrape and pinch again just to buy new shoes or a sweater for her sister or herself. She sighed heavily. At least Gabriella had a job now.

She grabbed a corner of the apron and wiped her eyes. That's right, Annie, she thought, feel sorry for yourself, but remember, it's not the end of the world.

Drawing a deep breath, she attacked the hardened crust on a fork. "I've lived through tough times before. Anyone can stick it out here for six months."

A load of soiled pots and pans took the place of the dishes

she'd washed. Her pulse settled down. She felt renewed confidence as she planned. While she was here, she'd put money in the bank. After all, the job included room and board.

Looking out the window, Annie saw Jake talking to another cowboy. Jake's not too hard to look at, she mused. He probably draws women like prime beef draws yellowjackets. Maybe she needed a Not To Do list with one entry—don't be attracted to the boss.

She watched him stride toward the corral, moving with the coiled power of a wild stallion—wonderful to watch from a distance, but dangerous up close.

Chapter Three

Annie shivered. *A wild stallion.* The thought of Jake's great horse, Bandit, sent another chill down her back. What was a woman afraid of horses doing on a ranch?

Drying her hands, she shifted her attention to the kitchen and planning her first meal for a crew of hungry cowboys.

She decided to let the new load of dishes soak while she brought in her luggage and changed into older clothes. With her small salary, she sure couldn't replace her one good outfit.

Jake forked another load of straw and manure into the wheelbarrow. He'd bailed out in a hurry, but he was haunted by the picture of Annie in the kitchen. He'd left her standing at the sink, dirty dishes piled high beside her, and her face still pale from shock.

Even from this distance, he heard the loud squeak of the screen door opening, and the quick tattoo of her high heels on the boards.

With his luck she'd light out toward town. He listened for the sound of her car engine as he checked a first-calf heifer.

Tomás tethered his bay just inside the barn and began to

unsaddle it. "The *señorita* is pretty," he said, working at the latigo on the front cinch.

"She still on the porch?" Jake feigned a nonchalance he was far from feeling.

"No. At her car with the trunk open."

If she's unpacking, she must be staying, he thought. The big question was how long would she stick around? "Give Miss Reed a hand with her baggage. I'll finish Big Red."

"You got it, boss," The lanky young Mexican cowboy ambled toward Annie and tipped his hat.

Jake bent to unbuckle the back cinch. Delighted feminine laughter drew his attention to the two people beside the car. Annie's face was alight with humor. Her bright curls bounced in the warm, fitful wind as it lifted, then plastered her skirt to her long, shapely legs. She said something that made Tomás laugh. He shouldered a cardboard box, and gestured for her to go ahead to the porch. Their cheerful voices floated back to Jake.

Dammit, he thought he'd made it clear her job was to cook, not get cozy with the men. Irritated, he lifted the saddle and swung it up onto a rack against the barn wall.

Another burst of conversation caught his attention. Annie backed out of the car holding a canvas bag, while the breeze molded her skirt to her neatly rounded bottom.

Jake's groin tightened. "Hell," he muttered, stripping off the rest of Big Red's rig. "Smartest thing is to keep way. Let her do her job."

Three hours later, Jake watched the ranch truck, its cargo bed still bare, pull to a stop, and a subdued driver climb out. "Kid, where's the fencing?"

"Sorry, boss." The young cowhand gave Jake a note, then tucked his thumbs in his jeans pockets and waited.

After a quick read, Jake crumpled the terse note, glaring at the empty pickup in front of the corral. His gut churned. Three words, one big problem. *No more credit.* Damn Larry Kendall.

He swung his attention to Steve.

"It's a damn shame." The young hand took off his cowboy

hat, and wiped his face. "Kendall gave me the note and told me to get lost."

Jake crammed the note into his pocket. "I'll talk to Kendall."

The young, brown-haired man went toward the bunkhouse with a muttered, "Kendall's a bastard."

Jake caught a whiff of tobacco and swung around as his top hand sidled up, smoking a thin, brown cigarillo. "Dammit, Travis. Ghostin' around'll get you blown to hell yet."

"Been there. Ate your chili." Travis's blond hair gleamed briefly as he doffed his wide-brimmed Resistol, smoothed his hair back, and set the hat back on his head. "Steve put a burr under your saddle?"

"Kendall's cut off my credit." Jake fired the balled-up note into the trash bin set just outside the barn. "I've never been late on a payment."

"Ben Russell's behind that."

Jake nodded. "Hell, they've worked together since kindergarten. Ben planned. Kendall did the dirty work. Still does."

Travis dropped his cigarillo on a bare patch of dirt, ground it out under his boot heel, then propped one shoulder against the barn doorjamb. "Like the times at school Larry or Ben'd egg you on to fight, then scream for a teacher when you did."

"I'd get punished twice, first at school and again at home." Jake shrugged. "Didn't stop me."

Travis chuckled. "In high school they said if Jake Stone didn't want to move, you could light a fire between his toes and he'd stare you down."

Jake raised an eyebrow. "Nobody tried."

"Ben still does. Just sneakier now."

"Been worse since Stephanie." Jake felt a slow surge of anger. "He couldn't keep her. Thinks he'll get my ranch. Change it into a playground for cowboy wannabes like his own. Give them a real chore and they'd disappear faster 'n a skunk can raise its tail."

"My money's on you, boss." Travis smoothed the red and white patterned bandanna around his neck. "See you hired a new biscuit-roller. Hope she cooks as good as she looks."

"Annie's here to work, not flirt. She signed a contract, but I give her a week before she cuts and runs."

"Maybe she'll fool you and stick around. Want me to encourage her?"

"Stay out of it." Jake stared at the house, remembering Annie's shocked expression when she saw the kitchen, then her laughter. "The mess didn't send her packing, but the job might."

"God, boss, your cookin's enough to make me puke. Hope she hangs around awhile."

"Don't get your hopes up. She's a city girl."

Jake watched his best friend stride toward a roan gelding hitched near the water trough. Travis had stood by him all through school. Still did.

Through the kitchen window, Annie watched one of the men lead his horse into the barn and saw Jake duck between the corral rails. He'd stopped in the house earlier to discuss wages and the meal schedule.

She retied her work apron, glad she'd had time to slip on comfortable jeans and a loose cotton T-shirt before clearing a space to start the meal.

Shaking her head at the work still ahead of her, she stirred the four pounds of hamburger sizzling in the Paul Bunyan-size frying pan. As she added enough chopped onions to bring an army to tears, the door to the mudroom at the end of the kitchen opened.

"Is that all you've done this afternoon?" Jake took off his hat, running lean, callused fingers through his hair as he looked around the kitchen. "It's not cleaned up."

Annie bristled. "Do you think I'm a miracle worker?"

"No, I thought you were a cook who wanted the job."

"The key word there is *cook*." She glared at him, automatically stirring the meat and onions. "I've been here four hours. It took most of that to scrub pans and find the counter top."

"I'll take your word for it, lady." He gestured toward the food. "Find what you need?"

"At least for dinner." She dumped in chili powder and two large cans of tomato paste, thinking she'd rather pour it over his hard head. "You've enough beef and pork in the freezer for three months, but we need fresh vegetables, fruits, more eggs, spices—"

"This is a ranch, not a health spa." He folded his arms and propped his hip against the counter. "Plain food's good enough. We'll eat at six, right?"

"You said six in the morning for breakfast, six at night for dinner." She added the two cans of Mexican corn she'd found behind a burlap bag dribbling pinto beans on the shelf. "Corn bread tamale pie is not fancy. I found canned fruit and a six-pound can of mixed vegetables. Those are the only halfway healthy things you have."

"Fixin' dessert?"

"In the oven."

Jake took a thick mug from the cupboard and began to fill it from the blue and white enameled pot set one end of the counter.

"Stop! That's not—"

"Where's the coffee?" he demanded, staring at the soapy stream.

"That junk? I dumped it. The pot needed a good scrubbing." She covered the simmering mixture on the stove with a heavy lid.

He moved closer. She tensed, grabbed the pot, added hot water, and washed it. "I'll make more. Where's the basket and filters?"

"Don't use 'em." He handed her the three-pound can of coffee. "Fill the pot with water and dump in coffee. We like it strong. A raw egg or shot of cold water will settle the grounds."

"Cowboy coffee?"

"Better than the dishwater city folk drink."

Annie laid the spoon on a small saucer. "I know my job, Mr. Stone. Get out of my kitchen and let me work."

"Bossy, aren't you?" Jake's green eyes held a hint of amusement when she glanced at him before opening the oven to peek at the two peach cobblers.

"Not bossy—honest. It'll be ready at six." She turned away from him, wiping the splattered stove. "Want the coffee right away or with supper?"

"When we eat."

From the corner of her eye, she saw him lean against the cold wood stove watching her. Uncomfortable, she moved father away to the pantry and grabbed the dry ingredients to make a corn bread topping. Why didn't he leave?

She threw him a glance over one shoulder. "Anything else, Mr. Stone?"

"What's the matter, Annie, nervous?"

"I'm busy." Opening a cupboard, she pretended to choose a mixing bowl.

His booted footsteps ambled across the kitchen. "Goin' into town. Be back for dinner."

Annie heard the door close behind him.

"Good riddance," she muttered, attacking the stack of dishes and pans she'd set to soak. The Blue Willow plate she lifted from the soapy water reminded her of her younger sister. Gabriella loved the pattern in blue with its two birds hovering over the arched Chinese bridge. Every time their mother changed jobs, Gabbie had carried a Blue Willow cereal bowl in her small suitcase to every new town, every new place.

Annie wondered how her younger sister liked her assignment in Australia. She rinsed a dish and stacked it in the drainer. Gabriella's university education had been worth the extra jobs they'd both worked.

Just before six o'clock, Annie heard the truck return and horsemen ride into the yard. Peering out the window, she saw Jake leave the truck, its bed filled with rolls of wire.

Other men unsaddled horses and rubbed them with thick gunny sacks. Masculine laughter carried to the house.

She turned back to check the food. The tantalizing odor of onions and chili hovered in the air mixing with the aroma of fresh perked coffee. Three bowls of rising bread dough, covered by clean dishtowels, added their yeasty fragrance from their positions on top of the unlit woodstove.

The outside mudroom door thumped. Through the inner door,

she heard water splash in the washbasin. She'd barely had time to open the oven and see if the pans of tamale pie and the garlic-buttered bread slices were done when Jake came in, face still damp. "Food ready?"

"Soon as your crew comes in."

Male voices and the clatter of booted feet heralded the arrival of Jake's cowhands in the dining area off the kitchen. Chairs scraped on the floor, and one deep voice exclaimed, "I'll be hornswoggled. A tablecloth?"

Another, younger-sounding cowhand chimed in, "Napkins and wildflowers?"

"*Sí.* The new cook put them there. Very pretty lady." Annie identified Tomás's richly accented voice.

"I'll be damned," the first speaker said, "A female belly robber."

Glancing at Jake, Annie mouthed, "Belly robber?"

He muttered, "Buck means cook. He's older than Methuselah, but he does a full day's work and nobody asks his age."

Jake grabbed a towel, wrapping it around the metal handle of the coffeepot. "I'll get this. Better feed 'em."

"Right away." Using two pot holders she'd brought in her cooking equipment, she picked up the first pan of corn bread-topped tamale and followed Jake through the door.

"Boys, meet Annie Reed."

The four tanned, broad-shouldered cowboys nodded politely.

"Annie, you've met Tomás. That's Steve next to him, Travis, and the old-timer's Buck."

She recognized Tomás. That meant the brown-haired, lanky young man beside him was Steve. She identified Travis as the tall blond in his mid-thirties. He smiled and gave her a jaunty salute. Next to him, the older man, Buck, grinned.

As she set the cheese and corn bread-covered pie on the table, the cowhands eyed the food dubiously.

Steve said in a low voice to Tomás, "What's that?"

Tomás muttered, *"Quien sabe.* Who knows?"

Annie rushed back to the kitchen for the rest of the food. When she set it on the table, the men were warily tasting the spicy meat pie.

Digging into her portion, she glanced at Jake. He chewed reflectively, then spooned more onto his plate, adding bread and vegetables.

Quiet filled the room except for the click of forks on plates, and the sounds of four hungry men eating.

Steve cleaned his plate and went back for seconds.

At the first taste, Buck's seamed and weathered face had broken into a roguish grin. Finally, he stood and bowed to Annie, folding her fingers in his callused hand. "Darlin', will you marry me?"

Delighted, she said, "You're too young for me, but thanks for asking."

Shrugging, Buck sat down and helped himself to a third serving of food. Travis beat him to it, piling a plate high with the spicy mixture.

Tomás used a chunk of bread to mop up his plate, and reached for the last helping.

"Hold your horses," Steve said, gripping the edge of the pan. "I'm stakin' my claim."

Annie smothered a grin as the two cowboys scowled at each other.

"I'll settle this." Jake reached across the table, deftly transferred the spicy mixture to his own plate, and ate it.

"Boss!"

Later, while Annie dished up the dessert, Travis announced, "Steve's goin' to the rodeo next month to see the palomino filly in the barrel races. What was her name again?"

"Mon-i-ca," Buck said in a singsong voice, his faded blue eyes twinkling. "Twenty years ago I'd a made a run at her myself."

"She wasn't born twenty years ago." Jake dug into a second serving of dessert.

Steve boyishly ducked his head, a deep red flooding his face.

Glancing at the other men, Annie said, "I saw a rodeo on TV last year. Are you a bronc rider?"

"Yes, ma'am." His chest swelled. "Ride bulls, bareback and saddleback broncs. Do calf-ropin', too."

"Isn't that dangerous?"

Steve straightened in his chair, his expression full of purpose. "Don't you worry, Miss Annie. I know what I'm doin'." He shoved his chair back. "Mighty fine grub." He sauntered from the room.

Tomás and Buck added their compliments and trailed out behind him.

Travis pushed his plate aside and said. "Best chow I've had." Wiping his mouth, the big blond took out a cigarillo and book of matches.

Annie frowned.

He eyed her. "Can I—may I smoke with my coffee?"

"I wish you wouldn't."

With a wink, he picked up his coffee mug and left.

She turned to Jake. "I didn't mean to chase him away."

"Don't worry. He'll sit on the porch."

Wearily, she gathered up plates and headed for the kitchen. To her surprise, Jake followed with more.

He stacked them on the counter. "I'll be in my office."

When the door closed behind him, Annie scanned the stacks of dirty dishes and pans ruefully. "Here I go again."

Sighing, she turned on the hot water. She had a mental picture of Gabbie laughing when she learned about her sister's first gourmet chef job on a working cattle ranch.

The next morning, she attacked the kitchen again. With all the dishes, pots, and pans scrubbed and put away, she swept the floor, and got down on her knees with a stiff brush and hot, soapy water to discover a well-worn oak plank floor under years of grime.

It took Annie a week to get the kitchen in order. With that done, she went out one morning after breakfast dishes were put away to work in the neglected herb and flower beds.

An hour later, Annie looked up from studying an old weed-filled garden at the side of the house to find Jake watching her.

"Grandma's kitchen garden," he said, tipping up the wide brim of his hat. "Dad and I kept it going for a while when I was a kid."

"The weeds have taken over." She watched him draw closer.

"I guess." His green eyes held her a moment longer.

She bent to pull another weed. "Did you want something?"

"Drank a cup of your good coffee just now. Had a handful of cookies, too."

She sat back on her heels. Her eyes were drawn to the well-worn denims hugging his muscular thighs. The way they fit left no doubt as to his masculinity. She looked away, embarrassed by her thoughts.

He tucked his thumbs in his front pockets. "Want to go horseback riding for half an hour?"

She tensed at the idea. "I've never been on a horse, and I don't plan to learn."

"C'mon, Annie." A shadow of irritation crossed his face. "I'll teach you. Living out here, you should know how to ride." He reached into his back pocket and brought out a small pair of gloves. "Buck got these when he went to town for the mail. I saddled Sage. She's gentle."

"You should've asked first. I'm not about to climb on top of some huge beast."

Impatiently, he slapped the gloves against one leg. "You're living on a ranch, Annie. We all ride."

"Not me." She picked up a trowel and dug into the soil. "Give me bike anytime. It'll go most places a horse can, and you don't have to feed it or clean up after it."

"Afraid?" he drawled.

She swallowed dryly. How could she explain? "I'm practical, not a coward. If I break my neck, you'll prop me up in the kitchen and order me to cook."

"Nope, just dock your pay." Moving closer, he offered a hand. "C'mon."

Still reluctant, she stood and brushed the dirt off her hands. "Give me time to wash up."

"Five minutes. I dug out some boots I wore when I was a kid. They're outside your room."

Less than five minutes later, they met on the porch and were headed toward the corral. Two horses waited, ears pricked forward, reins tied around the top fence pole. Clutching the

gloves Jake had given her, Annie stared at the black stallion.
"You'll ride Bandit?" she asked, forcing her voice not to
waver.

"Yeah. The buckskin's for you. She's a lady and has a
smooth gait."

Annie directed her unwilling attention to the smaller, light
brown horse with a black mane and tail. Close up, the mare
loomed huge, its back level with her chin. Annie's stomach
fluttered. How could she get up on the saddle? Why had she
agreed to try?

Jake spoke in a low tone. "Relax. Sage's watching. Act like
you've known horses all your life. If she thinks you're afraid,
it'll worry her. Make her jumpy."

She knew how the mare felt, Annie thought, as her arms
prickled with goose bumps. She felt Jake's warm palm against
the small of her back. His closeness made her even more skittish.

"I'll remember," she said, easing away from his hand.
"What next?"

"Pat her neck. Talk to her. Use her name. Let her get used
to you."

As Jake and Annie reached them, both horses whickered.
Bandit extended his nose toward Jake. He stroked the horse,
murmuring, "If Sage pokes her nose at you, go ahead and rub
it."

Annie wanted to run. Her legs trembled as she forced herself
to touch the mare's warm, dusky neck, saying in a low voice,
"Good horse. Nice Sage."

Sage nuzzled Annie's shoulder, and she froze, afraid to
breathe. Come on, chicken, she chided herself. Jake said this
horse is gentle.

With her body in tight control, Annie touched Sage's velvety
nose. Nothing happened, and she felt a little easier so close to
the mare—especially with a fence between them. Gradually,
Annie's confidence grew until the horse lowered its head and
touched her hair.

Should I move or stand still? Adrenaline charged through
her blood, setting up the urgent need to get away. Instead, she
clenched her fists and stood her ground.

The buckskin's warm breath washed across Annie's cheek. Its lips brushed her neck, then tugged on her collar.

She jumped back with a muffled shriek.

Sage threw up her head, pulling at the reins tethered to the fence.

"Whoa, girl." Jake moved in to calm the startled mare.

Nervously, Sage lifted her hooves, dancing in one spot. Jake placed a reassuring hand on her back and talked to her in a low voice.

Whinnying softly, Sage steadied.

"Try it again, Annie," Jake ordered. "Show Sage you're not afraid."

"Easy for you to say," she muttered, but followed his command.

Once the mare accepted Annie, Jake showed her where to grab the saddle's pommel and cantle, clasped her around the waist, and boosted her onto the horse's back.

Suddenly Annie was high off the ground with the vibrant mare standing steady under her. A fitful breeze, heavy with the odor of leather and horse, cooled her sweaty forehead and rippled her cotton blouse.

While Jake adjusted the stirrups, Annie tried to ignore his strong hands and the potent heat of his chest so close to her thigh. She reviewed his instructions, aware of a gathering excitement coursing through her blood. Still apprehensive of both horses, she discovered she wanted to ride beside him, see this land through his eyes.

He swung up onto Bandit. "Ready?"

"Ready as I'll ever be. I get nervous on a carousel pony."

His white teeth flashed as he tugged on the front brim of his hat. "Riding a horse is like having sex. It's the same motion, just not as pronounced."

His rare smile caused her pulse to gallop, and she hastily reminded herself of her Not To Do list.

Slowly they made a circuit of the corral, Jake's calm voice encouraging and coaching her. On the third time around, he stopped at the gate.

"Want to ride down to the valley floor?"

"It's your show," she said, her mouth dry with lingering fear. He opened the gate. She gently squeezed her knees against the mare's sides. Sage ambled through the opening, going faster once they'd cleared the corral.

Annie couldn't help clutching the pommel, shifting her weight. Sage took that as a signal to switch into a trot. Wildly, Annie tried to remember how to slow down her mount.

"Relax," Jake urged. He caught the reins near the buckskins's mouth, slowed both horses to a walk, and took the lead. Annie rode behind thinking she'd never get used to being on a horse.

At first, Annie kept her spine rigid, jolted by every step. She saw the easy way Jake sat, his body easy and fluid, rocking with the motion of his mount. She struggled to catch the rhythm of her horse. After a while, it became easier to stay in the saddle. A heady sense of accomplishment swept over her as they rode deeper into Rainbow Valley.

The trail wound along a gentle slope, shaded at intervals by sycamores and feathery-leafed tamarisks. Squirrels scolded from the trees. Leaves rustled. Powdery red dirt, churned by the passage of other horses, muffled the *clop* of Bandit's and Sage's hooves. In the sunny patches, the sweet pea fragrance from clusters of blue lupines rose in the warm air.

The trail widened, and Jake stopped. Annie joined him, looking across the wide brush and grass-filled range, dotted with russet cattle.

"What a view."

Jake shifted in the saddle, glanced at her, then gazed at the peaceful scene. "Most beautiful place on God's earth."

His rich, warm bass resonated deep within her, stirring her secret wish for a permanent place of her own. How would it be to ride across this valley beside him in all seasons, to stay here forever? No! Her future would not include Jake Stone or his ranch.

Annie rubbed her forehead with a gloved hand. Dismayed, she studied the smear of red earth on the heavy fabric. "Look, soiled already."

Jake's eyes narrowed. "You city people are all alike. A little dirt and you complain."

She raised her chin defiantly. "Buzz off, country boy. I didn't complain. I commented."

Reining her horse around, she saw a cluster of calves and their mothers just past the end of the sloping trail, and directed Sage down the rutted path.

She'd left Jake and his annoying presence behind. So far she'd stayed in the saddle. Her pleasure blossomed with her lessening dread of falling off the horse.

The sound of hooves indicated Jake was following.

"Eat my dust," she crowed.

Reaching the small herd, she watched two calves kick up their heels and race around their patient mothers. One baby shied at a small yellow butterfly, and dashed toward Annie's mount.

Instinctively, Annie pulled her foot out of the way of the frightened calf. Beginning to slide, she made a lunge for the pommel, but it was too late.

Jake yelled something about the stirrup. She yanked her foot out of it as she felt herself slipping, then landed on her back with a painful thud.

Black and white spots danced across her vision. She couldn't breathe, couldn't move. The bright desert sky above her pulsed dark and light in time to her heartbeat.

Spitting curses, Jake knelt beside her. "Dammit, Annie," he said in a rough tone, gently touching her legs and arms. "That was a fool stunt. Where does it hurt?"

It took her two tries to get the words out. "My back. Hard . . . to breathe."

"Stay still until we find out what's wrong."

"Wasn't . . . planning to dance."

His capable hands moved across her shoulders and down her ribs. "Nothing's broken here."

She caught one callused hand as it brushed over her breast. "That's not my back."

"Feisty, aren't you?" He sat back on his heels, his expression less grim.

She made a fist. "Want proof?"

With a faint smile, he shook his head. "I know when to back down."

Annie closed her eyes against the hot sunshine, and her growing attraction to the rugged man beside her. A dry, resinous breeze plucked at her blouse. The rocky ground under her was unyieldingly hard. A small stone poked her left hip. She took a cautious breath, let it out. Her lungs were working okay, but her back still ached. She moved her shoulders, arms, and legs, deciding she'd survived the fall intact.

"Annie?" A shadow fell across her closed eyelids. Warm fingers rested on her forehead. "Is there a problem?"

She opened her eyes. Jake was bent over her, his cowboy hat and broad chest shading her from the sun's rays. "Nothing a good soak in the tub won't cure," she said.

"Ready to sit up?"

At her yes he propped her up, and helped her stand. She clung to him, her legs wobbly as gelatin.

Chuckling, he held her closer. "Easy, there. We'll make a country girl of you yet."

"Takes more than one ride."

Nearby, Sage stood quietly beside Bandit. Both horses were ground-hitched, their reins trailing against the red soil and sparse grass.

Jake kept one arm around her as she limped to Sage.

Annie reached for the reins, apprehensive about riding again, but suddenly desperate to get away from Jake's virile scent and heat. She found herself trapped between the horse and his hard chest. As she looked into his eyes shaded by the Stetson, her heart pounded at their lambent gleam.

"Jake?"

Surely he didn't plan to kiss her.

"Annie, Annelise," Jake muttered, tipping her chin up with one blunt fingertip. In the bright spring sunlight his wide-brimmed hat cast an intimate shade across their faces.

His head dipped closer and her pulse raced.

"Dammit—" His mouth came down on hers, lips hard and exciting.

Chapter Four

Annie clenched her fist to pound on his back, but his potent kiss stopped her. Instead, she yielded as his lips gentled, inviting her into a sensual world. She felt the hot, wet heat of his tongue trace the seam of her lips. He tasted of coffee, of a working male's salty tang, and trouble.

He held her closer, one hand splayed between her shoulders, the other stroking down her back, molding her to his powerful body. She wrapped her arms around his ribs, caught in the spell of his primal heat and strength.

His long fingers curled under her bottom. Warmth pooled between her legs. No man had ever touched her like this. It was too much too soon, and she panicked.

"No." Annie jerked back, then hid her face against his soft denim shirt. She felt the press of pearl snap buttons along one cheek, the rasp of his callused fingers against her jeans, even his breath stirring her hair.

"Jake, we have to stop."

He clasped her shoulders, set her away, muttered an oath, and stepped back. Harshly, he said, "That kiss shouldn't've happened."

Something a little wild in her responded. He was so damned

controlled, while his kiss has completely shaken her. She gave him a cool smile. "We'll just pretend it didn't happen."

He suddenly looked taut, dangerous. "That easy for you, huh?"

"Why not?"

Once more she found herself wedged between his solid chest and Sage. A stirrup danced against her spine. His hard lips took hers in a kiss that scrambled her thoughts. She felt his powerful fingers cut her head. He slanted his mouth, nibbled, teased, aroused, until her knees threatened to give way. Then, as swiftly as he'd grabbed her, he released her.

Shaken by his unexpected move, Annie fought to catch her balance. "Listen," she said, straightening her blouse and hair. "Let's get this straight. I needed work. You wanted someone to cook decent meals for your men so they'd stay. I got what I wanted. So did you. We both know I'll be gone by the middle of September."

She looked past him at the two calves quietly nursing. "As you've been quick to point out, I'm a city girl and don't belong in the country."

"Yes, ma'am," he drawled, his expression blank, unreadable. "I'll stick to our contract."

Cautiously, Annie collected Sage's reins. Hoping the mare would follow her, she looked around for a small boulder to step up on and mount the horse.

"Need a boost?" Jake's strong hands circled her waist from the back. She arched away from him, halted by the bulk of the mare's broad side.

"Cooperate, Annie," he said in a flat voice. "We'll get home sooner."

She steeled herself against the rush of blood where his hands touched her, and silently acceded to his help.

The ride back up the trail felt far longer than the trip down. Her spine ached. Her legs burned, and she didn't want to think about sitting in a chair once they got back to the ranch.

Her mind kept returning to Jake's concern when he thought she'd been hurt, then his unexpected kiss. Still disturbed by her reaction, she rode in silence.

Half an hour later, back in the corral, Jake helped her dismount. Her senses, heightened from Jake's kiss, made her acutely aware of the pressure of his strong fingers on her waist and the mingled odors of horse and man. She could still taste him on her lips.

His gaze focused on her mouth with an intensity that made her nipples tighten. As she watched, he shuttered his expression.

Riveted to the patch of trampled earth, she fought to calm the emotions rioting through her soul. How could he shake her this way?

He turned away, stroked Sage's nose, then bent to undo the latigo on the saddle.

Bewildered by his hot-and-cold attitude, Annie pushed through the corral gate, closed it, and stumbled up the shaded dirt path toward the house. Why had she let him kiss her a second time?

Strength flowed back into her body as her temper rose. "Catch me by surprise, huh? It won't happen again," she told herself. Reaching the scraggly lawn, she kicked a small rock off the narrow track into the flower bed. Jake was just too damned sure of himself. She bent down and yanked a weed from the roses beside the front steps.

"Talkin' to the wind?" Travis's soft query from the porch caught her unawares.

"No." She marched up the wooden stairs. "I was talking to Jake." She passed him by—gratified by the heavy clatter of her boot heels on the thick planks—and slammed open the screen door.

She heard Travis chuckling. He followed her into the kitchen. "Brought my thermos for tomorrow's lunch. Goin' into Prescott on business. I'll be gone all evening."

She eyed him as he set the stainless steel cylinder on the counter. "What's so funny?"

Casually he leaned against the kitchen table and grabbed a handful of cookies. "First time I saw a gal spittin' mad over a friendly ride."

"He caught me by surprise and kissed me." She couldn't

believe the words had popped out of her mouth. That's what she got for giving in to temper.

At Travis's grin, she added, "Well, he did."

"Jake force you?"

Remembering the hot, sensual touch of his mouth on hers, she said, "Get real. Force, no. Trick, yes."

Travis studied her a moment, his expression growing serious. "Tickles me to hear it. He's been a damned hermit. Works himself too hard."

"I know. In the short time I've been here, he's always busy, even after dinner."

"You could get him to take a break." Travis examined the cookie in his hand. "He needs a woman to care for him."

Annie crossed her arms, trying to hide her aching response to Travis's suggestion. No. way could she get involved with Jake. "I work here. That's all."

"You've done a helluva lot more. Jake don't normally take off to go ridin' for pleasure. He did today."

Travis moved toward the door, his ornate spurs jingling. He adjusted his hat and paused, piercing Annie with a look. "Jake's the best friend a man or woman can have—or the worst enemy. He doesn't forgive or forget."

Jake had watched Annie stalk up the path, speak to Travis, then go into the house. He'd curbed his desire to follow her. No city girl could dangle him at the end of her lasso. He ran his tongue across his lips, and tried to ignore the feelings she aroused in him. Damn, it was like drinking from a spring-fed pool in a hot desert wind.

He finished unsaddling the buckskin and groomed her. If only Annie was a ranch girl, one who could accept the hard times and avoid the dangers.

Jake ran a hand down each of the mare's legs, remembering his first quick shot of fear when he saw Annie fall. She'd been game about that experience, joking in spite of landing hard on her back. But it proved she was too vulnerable for ranch life.

"Hell," he muttered, releasing Sage into the corral. "One more problem to keep me awake."

That evening, while Annie finished dinner preparations, Jake joined her in the kitchen. Reaching for a glass in the upper cupboard, he brushed her shoulder. She jerked away, confused by her throbbing response to his accidental touch.

"Getting clumsy, Mr. Stone?"

Jake sighed and rubbed the back of his neck. "Annie, I'm not gonna jump you."

She picked up her Sabatier serrated knife and sliced more bread. "You mean I won't have to sleep with my boning knife under the pillow?"

"Hell, no." He twisted the cold water faucet, stuck his glass under the stream, and moodily watched it fill.

"Good." She piled the sliced bread in a bowl, covering it with a cloth. "You don't look like fish or fowl, anyhow." When he studied her through narrowed eyes, she added, "But you *are* in a foul mood."

He groaned, and set his empty glass on the counter with a sharp click. "Annie, please, no puns."

"Sorry. I'll try to curb the urge."

"Do that." He stalked out.

Annie bit her lip, wondering why she had to make jokes when she got nervous.

She'd tried to establish a light, joking tone around Jake, but her traitorous body still remembered the heat generated by his touch, his kiss. It was going to be a long five months.

Hours after the crew had finished dinner and scattered to their own activities, she saw the light on in Jake's office.

He sat at the computer, his profile to her. A parchment-shaded floor lamp spread a pool of light across the work area. She watched him study the screen, then wipe his eyes. His normally erect back was slightly bent. Even from where she stood, he looked tired.

"I brought you coffee."

He jerked and slowly faced her. "Sounds good."

Setting the tray on a table between two chairs in front of the stone fireplace, she nodded toward a pile of file folders and open envelopes stacked at one end. "Looks like you need a break."

"I could use one." He stood and stretched. Muscles bunched and rippled under his worn denim shirt. She recalled the feel of his hard chest against her breasts that afternoon, and almost groaned. He was too damned virile for her peace of mind.

Jake slumped in a chair across the low table from her, swallowed some coffee, then leaned his head back and closed his eyes. "You're a lifesaver."

She cleared her throat. "You look tired. Can I help?"

"You just did. A jolt of caffeine will clear my head." He studied her through half-open eyes. His thick, dark lashes added to the impression of a lazy panther assessing his prey.

Annie mentally shook herself. "I meant do you need help sorting or filing records?"

He raked a hand through his hair and looked at her with a wry smile. "How about a lucky rabbit's foot or a magic lamp?"

Relieved, she smiled. "If I had the lamp, what would you wish for?"

"A hundred thousand dollars would do it."

"Might as well say a million."

"I'll take it." With a faint smile, he reached for a brownie and took a generous bite. "Things've been tight since my dad died."

She kicked off her shoes and tucked her legs up under her, wincing at the unaccustomed soreness.

Jake gave her a knowing look. "How you doin' after your fall today?"

"Just a couple of bruises. It's the ride that made my muscles stiff."

He drank some coffee, his shadowed eyes studying her over the mug's rim. "Each time you go riding, it'll get easier. But don't go alone. If I can't be with you, take Buck."

"Don't worry, I'm not planning any more rides."

He set his mug on the table and leaned forward. "One of your duties at roundup will be to follow the crew into the high country and cook a hot meal for them. Only way in is by horse.''

Annie gulped. Her palms grew clammy as anxiety spun through her body. Somehow she had to conquer her fear of horses.

The growl of a powerful engine broke the tense silence. Jake reached the window in a few swift steps. Annie followed, curious, but not worried.

As she reached Jake's side, she saw Travis's black four-by-four swing into its usual spot, overshoot, and stop, the front bumper nudged against the thorny canes of an ocotillo.

"Drunk," Jake muttered, sounding surprised.

Travis climbed out and clung to the door.

Annie felt a quick slash of concern. "Jake, it looks like he's injured."

"He is." Swearing, Jake strode out the door, down the steps, and met the man staggering toward them.

As she followed Jake, Annie flipped on the porch light and saw a dark line of blood trickling from the corner of Travis's mouth. One eye was swollen shut. He held a bloodied hand against his side.

Jake slipped an arm around his friend, steadying him.

Annie heard Travis catch his breath, then say, "Watch it. Think they cracked a rib."

"Who?" Jake supported him up the stairs and into the kitchen.

"Cutter and a couple of his drinking buddies."

Annie's stomach tightened in cold, sick nausea when she got a better view of Travis's injuries. "That's awful."

Travis grinned at her and Jake, then cursed, dabbing at his cut lip. "Thought they had me. They guessed wrong."

Listening to their conversation, Annie forced her hands to stop shaking as she opened the medical box and filled a basin with warm water.

In the meantime, Jake had eased the battered cowboy into a chair. Now, one shoulder braced against the door frame, he watched from his vantage point.

She bathed the cuts on Travis's face, saying, "A doctor should check you in case something's broken."

"Naw, I don't need a doctor." Travis gingerly touched his left side. "Jake can wrap my ribs like he did when that old boss cow charged me."

"Had to." Jake's tone said it was no big deal. "Caught that bunch of herd-quitters a day's ride out."

"So, do it again." Travis shrugged, muttered a soft oath, then half-smiled at Annie through swollen lips. "Be a darlin', and fish a smoke outta my pocket."

"Why? So you can stink up my kitchen? Forget it." She rested a hand on his forehead. "You're not running a fever, are you?"

"Cut it out, Annie," Jake said. "He doesn't need your hands all over him. This isn't the first fight he's been in."

"You can go to hell, Jake Stone. He's hurt." She opened the freezer compartment.

"Come on, boss. Lay off." Travis stared at Jake.

Jake crossed his arms, glaring at the injured man. "Forget her. What the hell happened? How'd you get crosswise to Cutter in Prescott?"

"Rosie and me had a date to go to the Red Bull for a steak and dancing." He smiled at Annie, his puffy lips making his mouth lopsided. "We've gone together for a couple of months."

Travis shrugged. "Made a trip to th' john. When I came out, she was dancin' with Cutter. I stepped in and Cutter punched me, so I decked him. His friends jumped me."

He glanced at Annie, then back to Jake. "Two months of Rosie. Hell, I thought I'd finally found me the right woman."

"And didn't you?" Annie asked.

"Last I saw, she had Cutter's head on her lap." Travis put one hand to his ribs, muttering, "Damn, that hurts."

Jake's expression hardened. He pushed away from the door frame and rested one hand on his friend's shoulder. "Wise up. I learned years ago no woman's worth fighting for."

* * *

Annie woke to the persistent beep of the alarm clock.

It was still dark. She pushed back the covers and stood on the braided rug. Dreams had tormented her all night. Dreams of Jake saying, "No woman's worth fighting for."

Half an hour later, the cinnamon scent of rolls mingled with the aroma of fresh brewed coffee, plump sausages, and bacon. At the big stove, she fried three eggs each for the hungry crew.

Buck sauntered into the kitchen. His bowed legs testified to years spent on horseback.

"Mornin', Annie," he drawled, snagging a hot cinnamon bun. "Gut-busters again?" He sniffed at the bun in his hand and rolled his eyes. "Gawd, that's fit for the gods."

She handed him a plate piled with crisp bacon and sizzling sausages. "Put this on the table, Buck. I'll bring the rest."

In two trips, she served everyone and took her place. After one, quick assessing glance in her direction, Jake became the hard-nosed boss, ignoring her as he rapped out orders to the hands. By the time he laid his fork down and stood, even Buck had ceased his banter.

Breakfast was quick and silent.

She'd just hung up her apron, when she heard someone washing up in the mudroom. Jake came in drying his face.

He sent an unreadable look in her direction, and poured himself a glass of cold lemonade from the jug in the refrigerator.

"You've been hard at it for hours. Why don't you let someone help?"

"Can't." He took a big swig of lemonade. "Stock has to be tended, and the men are already doubling up on work."

Abruptly, he turned toward the door, motioning for her to follow.

Annie's heel caught on the doorsill. Jake's solid arm whipped around her waist, keeping her upright.

She had the sudden urge to lean against him, amazed to find his mingled scents of hard-working man and horse didn't repel her. The heat of his strong body stirred uneasy feelings. For a moment she lost track of where she was. A warm breeze filled with the earthy odors of cattle and new grass whispered through the porch columns, rippling her skirt and blouse.

"Annie." He released her and moved to the railing. "See? That's what's important—Rainbow Valley."

Wary of his unexpected effect on her, she joined him, scanning the valley floor and the land rising in giant steps to blue and purple mountains in the distance. Captivated by the scene, she murmured, "I can see why."

"No one will take my land." She heard the echo of old pain and new determination in his words.

"Who would do that? It belongs to you."

"Russell's been after if for years."

A plume of dust puffed up behind trees screening the road, and Jake said, "Someone's coming."

The white and gold Range Rover crested the hill and stopped beside Annie's car. When Ben Russell stepped out, an uneasy chill crept over her.

She heard Jake's low curse as the burly, expensively dressed man sauntered toward them with the air of a buyer surveying his potential purchase.

"State your business and leave." Jake's wide-legged stance took on a subtle menace.

"You know what I want—this ranch." Russell tipped back his creamy gray Stetson. "Word is you're about tapped-out. I'll settle for Wild Rose Canyon—for now."

Jake, his fists bunched, moved to the top of the porch stairs. "It's not for sale."

"That will change." Ben made a dismissive gesture with one hand, turning his attention to Annie.

"Cutter saw you with Jake. Said you were here." Russell's arrogant grin broadened. "Decided on my offer, sweet thing?"

"I gave you my answer." She glanced at Jake's tense expression. "I'm working for Mr. Stone now."

Ben stepped closer to the bottom tread of the porch. "He can't offer you the same advantages I can."

Russell's gaze moved to Jake. She saw the flash of hatred in his eyes. Then it was gone, replaced by a lazy, self-satisfied smirk. "Gonna settle for my leavings again, Stone?"

Leavings? Annie moved uneasily. What did he mean?

Jake vaulted down the stairs, landing nose to nose with Russell. "You better haul your ass outta here if you value your hide."

Ben stumbled backward. "Touch me and I'll sue."

"You're trespassing, Russell." Moving with swift, coiled power, Jake closed the gap between them. "Stay off my land, and don't bother Annie. Like she said, she works for me now."

Shouting more threats, Ben stomped to the Rover, yanked the door open, and stopped.

Jake planted himself between Annie and the beefy man. She shuddered. Ben Russell made her skin crawl.

Even from a distance, she felt the cold impact of Ben's inspection. He smoothed the beaded fringe of his vest, saying, "Stone tell you about his wife?"

His wife? The breath caught in Annie's throat. Not that she cared, but was Jake married? He sure didn't act like it.

Jake fought the urge to plant a fist in the middle of Russell's malicious grin. The creep touched the brim of his hat, and drove off.

Behind him Annie cleared her throat. "Why did he talk about your wife? You said you weren't married."

"I'm not—now." He noticed she'd put more space between them, and felt a twinge of regret. His voice harshened as he asked, "What advantages did Russell mean?"

Annie traced the porch rail with one finger. "He interviewed me for a chef's job. The big jerk made a different kind of offer."

Scowling, Jake leaned against a post beside the stairs and crossed his arms. "Bet I know what he wanted. He won't bother you with the hands and me here. Just stay off his land and out of his way."

She met his gaze straight on. "I told you when you hired me, I don't want to go near that snake again."

Two days later, Jake and his crew had been out on the range all day when the phone rang. Annie answered the one on the small table beside the staircase, startled to hear a familiar voice.

"Darryl, how did you find me?"

"You have a talky friend at the local cafe. Figured they'd have heard of you there in a town that small."

"You must've talked to Verna."

"That was the name." Hearing her friend's voice brought back happy memories of classes together at the Culinary Institute. "Beth okay? Did she have the baby?"

"We have a two-week-old daughter, Melissa Ann." The young father's voice held intense pride.

"Wonderful. Where are you all living now?"

"That's the reason I'm calling." Darryl's tone was serious. "Beth and the baby are living in Kansas with Beth's parents."

He hesitated, and Annie sensed his uneasiness even over the telephone. "Annie, I heard you tried for the job at Sunrise Peaks and ended up on a cattle ranch." He cleared his throat. "I . . . the truth is I'm in Prescott at a motel. I start as chef at Sunrise Peaks tomorrow."

"Russell's ranch?"

"Yes." He sighed. "I heard you applied for the position and didn't get it. You're more qualified than me, but I took the job anyway because I had to get a decent salary. God, Annie, I'm in a big mess. Russell doesn't know I'm married, and he thinks I graduated from the Culinary Institute."

"Can't you tell him the only reason you dropped out before the last few courses was to support Beth when she got pregnant?"

"He'd fire me before I worked a day. He thinks he's getting a single guy who'll flirt with the female guests and prepare *haute cuisine* on demand. I need this job."

Hearing the desperation in his voice, she said, "I won't tell anyone. I'm glad you warned me."

"Beth said you'd keep the secret." Her ex-classmate cleared his throat again. "One more thing. Russell wants a special dessert for tomorrow night."

Annie frowned. "That shouldn't be a problem. You've learned lots of good recipes. How about Cherry Tart *Flambée*, or use apricots instead. Torch that baby. Knock their socks off."

"Too ordinary. Russell's wants something different, sophisticated. The princess of Darzakan will arrive tomorrow. He wants to impress her. He said to fix the kind of thing you'd see at *Les Masters du Chocolat* competition. I can't do that, but *you* can."

"Darryl, you're a good chef. Improvise."

"But I never took the advanced course! C'mon, Annie. Be a pal and help me make something."

"I can't. Ben Russell's a jerk. He scares me."

"What? Am I talking to the same redheaded fury who once poured ice water over that guy who hassled Beth?"

"That's me. Same person. Different problem." Annie sank onto the second step and leaned her cheek against the cool wood banister. "My boss and Russell hate each other. I signed a six-month contract. I won't irritate Jake by going to Peaks Ranch."

"Don't tell him." Darryl sounded on the edge of panic. "Park off the ranch road in some trees and walk to the kitchen door. Anyone stops you, pretend you're a guest."

Annie felt her resolve melt. When her old car had blown a head gasket, Darryl had repaired the car and kept it running. Beth had cheered her on, and assisted her in finding another job after her final run-in with Chef Franco.

"Just get me started with a fabulous dessert. I'll take it from there."

Annie felt her throat tighten at the prospect of being on Russell's place, but she couldn't say no to Darryl. "All right. Do they have a convection oven?

"Russell had the kitchen redone." Relief colored Darryl's voice. "You're a lifesaver, Annie. When I call Beth and tell her, she'll be grateful, too."

"Hey, we're friends," Annie said, uncomfortable with his gratitude. "How about Chocolate Decadence Cake with Raspberry Sauce? You can make that ahead of time. Bake the cake in the morning. I'll meet you at Russell's in the afternoon and do part of the ganache glaze, chocolate band, and sugar rose." She hung up and stared out the window.

At that moment, the independence she'd relied on since she

was eight years old reasserted itself. Jake didn't own her. Once she finished her work after lunch, there was no reason she shouldn't go.

As if conjured up by her thoughts, she heard the stamp of booted feet on the porch and Jake's voice edged by impatience. "Dammit, Steve, how'd you let Cutter back you into this corner?"

They came through the door, letting it slam behind them.

"Boss, how should I know he wanted me to ride broncs bareback at the Peaks ranch tomorrow afternoon to show off for the dudes? I thought he meant at the rodeo next month."

They stopped, Jake with his back to her. "Kid, you know there's bad blood between Ben and me. Go ahead tomorrow, but that's it. From now on, anybody who works for me had better steer clear of Russell's place."

The next day, Jake reined in Bandit at the top of a low rise where two tamarisk trees made a thin shade. He studied the hint of trouble that had brought him to this vantage point. A haze of dust rose in the west section of Rainbow, as if cattle were being rounded up. They shouldn't be. He'd settled a herd of nursing cows and their calves there because of the rich grazing and a spring-fed pond.

A few minutes' ride brought him to a row of windbreak trees. He cursed at the scene spread out in front of him. Cattle milled in aimless confusion. Cows separated from their calves called, answered with frantic bawls. Two dudes on horseback with lariats practiced trying to lasso whatever animal they could reach. Two other cowboy wannabes stood holding the horses' reins and studying a young calf stretched out on its side. Nearby, the mother moved restlessly, ready to charge. Jake couldn't blame her.

He kicked Bandit into a gallop. The greenhorns wheeled to face him, scrambled up on their mounts, and hightailed out of there toward Russell's ranch. He wanted to chase them down and beat the hell out of them, but the injured calf came first.

* * *

"This is the last one." Annie wrapped a chocolate band around the miniature dark-chocolate-on-chocolate cake. She added the swirl of raspberry coulis along one side, and slid the candy rose and twin green leaves on top.

Darryl set the rich dessert beside the other ones. "You saved my job, Annie. You're a real pal."

"You owe me, big time." She glanced at the clock. "Got to hustle back to the ranch and start cooking."

After peeking out the door, she slipped through and sidled along one wall. Just as she reached a corner of the building, she heard Russell and another familiar voice coming from the yard.

"Jake?" she muttered. What was he doing here?

He could barely contain his fury, that much was clear. "I don't give a rat's ass about your dudes," he yelled at Russell. "Keep them off my land, away from my herd, or I'll have 'em arrested for trespassing and I'll sue you!"

Russell blustered, "Cause problems for my guests, Stone, I'll have Sam Morgan throw your ass in jail!"

"You heard me. I'll beat the crap outta the next one hassling my cattle."

The click of his horse's hooves coming closer warned Annie in time to step behind a thick stand of oleanders. Hidden by the branches, she watched Jake ride past, his expression cold and hard.

Her breath whooshed out in relief. Thank heaven he hadn't seen her. She wouldn't want to face him any time soon. He'd be furious.

Screened by sagebrush between her and the ranch road, she crept to where she'd left the car. One more curve and she'd be there, safe.

Keys in hand, she reached the car when a deep, frigid voice drawled, "Take th' wrong turn, Annie?"

Chapter Five

Startled, Annie straightened and slowly faced Jake, plunging her hands into the pockets of her cotton slacks. "That's none of your business."

"It is when I find my cook on *this* ranch." The saddle creaked as he shifted his weight. The hard glint in his eyes was meant to be intimidating. "Fishin' for a better deal, or lookin' for a lover?"

"You don't trust me, do you?"

"About as far as I can throw my Aberdeen Angus bull." He tightened the reins as Bandit sidestepped. "Get supper by six like I hired you to do." He wheeled and rode away.

Annie watched him go. What a big, bad cowboy he thought he was. Who had died and made him God?

Driving toward the fork in the road that would take her to Rainbow Ranch, she thought about Jake's comment. If she didn't know better, she'd say he'd acted jealous. But why on earth—? She dismissed the idea and turned her attention to the argument she'd heard. It sounded like some of the Sunrise Peaks guests had chased his cattle. She remembered the first time she'd met him, and the small herd that had escaped through a gate left open by a Peaks guest.

It shouldn't make any difference to do her, but she did care. Seeing Jake's love for his land, and the hours of hard work he put into the ranch, had already won her admiration.

"Wake up, girl." She reminded herself she'd be leaving in the fall to do find a job where she'd gain recognition in her field. Someday she'd attain security as a world class chef. Then she wouldn't have to depend on Jake Stone or anyone else.

What happened to Jake and his ranch wasn't her concern.

"That woman's a pain in the butt," Jake muttered, as he studied the faint hoofprint. Two weeks had passed since he'd encountered Annie at Russell's place. Since then she'd avoided him. But why? What was she hiding?

He couldn't fire her anyway, he mused, touching the front curve of the print. The crew would rebel. Hell, they treated her like a sister. Now, according to Buck, she'd said, "Someone find Jake and give the grump his lunch before he starves." Buck said he'd laughed at the joke and ridden out to check fences. He hadn't expected Annie to saddle up and ride out, because she was still spooked by horses.

Jake straightened and brushed the red dirt off his hands. He'd recognized the pattern made by Sage's horseshoe. Annie always rode the buckskin when she went out on horseback with him to practice riding.

"My lunch." He cursed himself because he'd ducked out without stopping to grab it. He had to find her before she got into trouble. Anything could happen.

He swung into the saddle, following Sage's tracks. Damn her, why didn't Annie keep her nose in the kitchen where she belonged?

The prints led toward the herd of cows and nursing calves in the west pasture. He'd put an old boss cow in there to guard the young mothers and their offspring from Ben's guests. She'd charge anyone not on horseback.

Jake kicked Bandit into a canter. If Annie stayed on her horse, she'd be safe. But if she dismounted or was thrown— He leaned forward, urging his horse into a gallop.

The windbreak loomed ahead. Sage's hoofprints pointed straight toward it. Bandit soared over the split-rail fence, sped between the dark trunks, and scattered a small band of cows.

Jake reined in, his attention fixed on the buckskin peacefully drinking at the pond. Where the hell was Annie?

He stood in his stirrups and scanned the pasture.

"Annie!" His shout startled a young calf who shied away, ran a few steps in the thick grass, then returned to its mother.

Jake listened for an answer in the calm, warm air.

He called again.

"Up here." The yell came from a low-growing cottonwood near the pond. A flash of yellow in the thick leaves caught his attention.

"Hey, Sherlock, I'm up here in the tree."

Jake's tense muscles eased. He located Old Sin, the boss cow, halfway around the wide pond peacefully chewing its cud.

Annie perched on a thick branch, relaxing against the trunk.

"Practicin' to be a bird?" he drawled.

She glared at him. "Your mean-tempered cow chased me."

"That's her job. She protects the herd. Put 'er here two weeks ago." Frowning, he studied her precarious position. "How'd you get up there?"

"I sure didn't fly." She slowly swung her feet, looking at home in her green bower. "Good thing this cottonwood was close, and I still remember how to shinny up a tree. I was scared to death when that ugly beast charged."

She shifted her position, causing a light shower of twigs and leaves. "Keep that vicious cow away. I'll get down."

"Deal." He kicked loose of one stirrup, ready to slide off and catch her. She might be a city girl, he thought, but she knew her way around a tree.

When she came within reach, he circled her waist with one arm and settled her in front of him.

"I'm taking you home."

"Get me to my horse. I'll ride Sage back to the house. At least I'm used to her."

"You in charge now? We'll ride double until it's safe."

Tightening his grasp, he felt the warmth of flesh through her bright yellow blouse. It invoked the fantasy of her naked and welcoming in his bed. She smelled of sunshine and spring flowers. He had the wild impulse to bury his face in her soft curls, to taste the silken band of skin where her neck curved into her shoulder. With a suddenness he hadn't experienced since his teens, he wanted her—now—on the grass—in his arms, skin against skin.

She shifted in the tight wedge between the pommel and his fly. He smothered a groan. "Sit still, Annie, before you start something I'll want to finish."

"Than put me down."

"Can't. Old Sin hates anything on two feet. Wanna play tag with her again?"

He silently cursed the growing heaviness in his loins. A few minutes more of this and he'd be howling at the sky like a randy coyote.

He grabbed Sage's reins. "You can switch beyond the wind-break."

She looked over her shoulder. "Well, let's do it."

His pulse kicked up another notch. He eased Bandit and the buckskin into a walk. Each fluid motion of Annie's bottom stroked his hypersensitive flesh. Damn, he ached.

Suddenly, Annie sat taller and glanced over her shoulder. Jake knew she felt the bulge testing the metal buttons on his fly.

In desperation, he estimated the distance to the tamarisks and safety.

Twenty paces—he gritted his teeth. A sharper bounce—he could almost hear the buttons groan.

Ten paces—did one just pop? Annie's rump pressed against the critical spot. *Damn.*

Five paces—Apache torture? "Get a grip," he muttered, then choked on the image.

"Excuse me? On what?"

"Nothing." He tightened his hold on her waist, his thumb nestled under the curve of one breast. If he moved that thumb a little higher—

"Jake, we've passed the trees. Do we change now?"

"Not yet. We'll go left to the gate and cross through. It's safer." But not for me, he thought. Not with his senses filled with Annie's fragrance, the feel of her body, the sound of her voice. What would happen if he bent his head and sampled the soft skin of her throat, traced her ear with his tongue, or nuzzled the nape of her neck? He imagined lifting and turning her, fitting his mouth against hers, exploring the texture of her teeth—and the dark, honeyed heat that lay beyond. Her firm breasts would move against his chest, and her thighs would cradle him intimately—and, hell, where'd that come from?

He shifted one leg to ease the strain. Bandit danced uneasily.

"Jake!" Annie leaned back clutching his arm.

He sucked in a lungful of air. "Damn it, Annie, don't move. Another stunt like that and you'll do serious damage."

She froze in place for a moment, before easing forward. "Make your horse behave, or put me down so I can get on Sage," she said in a toneless voice.

"Ready to go another round with Old Sin?" He urged Bandit toward the gate. "She's the ornery critter that stove in Travis's ribs."

Annie's fingers trembled against his arm. "Fine. Just hurry."

Pure, old-fashioned frustration touched off the anger he'd felt from the moment Buck said she'd gone out alone. "Why in sweet hell did you ride out here?" Bending from the saddle, he opened the gate, tugged Sage through, then closed it.

"Put me down."

Reining in Bandit, he swung off, ground-hitched both horses, and stepped back.

It took several attempts for her to stretch far enough to slip a foot into the stirrup. Impatient, and touchy with arousal, he clamped his hands around her waist, hoisting her from the saddle.

"I can do it myself," she protested, prying at his fingers.

Abruptly, he released her. She took a step, wavered, and grabbed the stallion's saddle, her face suddenly pale.

Silently cursing his own stupidity, he went down on one knee in front of her to examine the foot she was favoring.

"Why didn't you tell me you'd been hurt?" he demanded, easing her boot off to examine her ankle and foot.

"And give you the pleasure of saying 'I told you so'?" She braced her hands on his shoulders. "Lead Sage over here, or get out of my way."

"After I wrap that foot."

An hour later, Annie rode up the dirt trail past the line of shade trees into the corral. Bending her head to fiddle with the reins, she peered at her silent companion from the corner of her eye. His hat shaded most of his expression, except for his lips, set now in a grim line.

Earlier, he'd had the same expression when he opened the first aid kit tied behind his saddle, grabbed a roll of elastic bandage, and smoothed it around her foot.

Jake dismounted and led both animals into the cool shade of the barn. He plucked her off the saddle and set her on a closed storage chest.

"Stay here, where you can't get into trouble," he ordered, reaching for the lunch tied behind the buckskin's cantle. "I'll unsaddle Sage and rub her down before we go up to the house."

She pushed to her feet, keeping most of the weight on her uninjured left foot. "I rode Sage. I'll take care of her." Swallowing, she forced herself to lay one hand on the mare. "I know what to do."

"Sure you do, just like you knew what you were doing in Old Sin's territory." While he answered her, he'd released the various straps and ties. Handing her the insulated lunch pack, he lifted the saddle and swung it onto a rack.

Knowing how heavy the saddle was, she was torn between admiration and the irrational desire to punch him. "If you won't let me—"

"Forget it, Annie. Sit over there."

Apparently determined to ignore her, he turned back to Sage.

If that was his attitude, she had better things to do than sit here and play poor, pitiful female. With that thought, she limped out of the barn and up the dirt path toward the house. Pausing on the shaded portion of the path, she rested her foot and looked west—between the sycamores—to the valley and the ridge beyond. Leaves on the shade trees hung motionless in the noonday heat. A few birds called to each other. Distant sounds of cattle and horses carried to her.

Without warning, Jake spoke from close behind her. "Don't follow orders worth a damn, do you?"

Before she could answer or protest, he scooped her into his arms. Quelling an urge to rest her cheek against his worn denim shirt, she stiffened.

"You can put me down now," she said quietly. "Nothing's broken. I just twisted my foot on a stone."

"And it hurts like hell to walk." A wry smile kicked up one corner of his mouth. "Been there myself."

He tightened his grip under her knees and across her back. "Annie, relax. It won't hurt to let me get you over the rough spots."

"You're the boss," she murmured. How had he changed from the tight-lipped, furious man to this tender cowboy in an instant, she wondered, looking up to meet his eyes. They'd taken on a new, softer light. She found herself drawn to them, to the man who held her, the one who eased her pain. Sliding one hand up to his shoulder, she felt the play of muscles under her fingers.

He shifted his grasp, drawing her closer. She laid her head against him, hearing his strong heartbeat under her cheek, enveloped in his strength, feeling cherished.

They moved through the dappled shade into bright sun as he strode up the path. Then they were up the stairs and into the house.

"That foot needs ice," he said, settling her in one corner of the couch, with her back against the pillows. Carefully, he tucked a pillow under the injured foot, then got an icepack from the kitchen.

He sat on the edge of the couch, one hard hip against her upper thigh. He eased the ice into position, then his green eyes searched her face. "Better?"

Nodding, she studied his expression for any clue to how he felt. His nearness made her breath catch in her throat. He was so damned overpoweringly male.

As he rubbed one hand across his face, she glimpsed—for a moment—the vulnerable man behind his tough exterior.

"Thanks, Jake." She touched a tiny scar on his cheek, then pulled her hand back. "I'm sorry. While I looked for you, I saw the moms and their babies, and remembered what you'd said about the dudes hurting a calf. I just wanted to get close to the one you'd doctored. I didn't realize the old cow would charge me."

Annie saw the lines around his mouth deepen. Nervously she rattled on. "When the cow snorted and lowered its head, I finally got the picture. I made a run for the tree, but twisted my foot, so I jumped for a lower branch one step ahead of her. I—"

His lips caught hers with a hunger that shattered her false composure. She clung to his shoulders, her whole being focused on the pleasure of his mouth against hers, his strong body arched over her. He cradled her cheek in his hand, stroked his tongue against her lips, and deepened the kiss.

The hot ache in her foot, the freezing ice against her skin, the earlier fear when Old Sin charged her, all disappeared under the power of Jake's touch. She curled one hand around the back of his neck and rode the shattering, sensual waves he generated. He sank lower, his arm brushing her sensitive nipple as he changed the angle of their kiss. Heat from his vibrant body flowed around her. She wanted, *needed* him against her to ease the ache centered deep within.

Beyond words, she spread her other fingers along his spine and urged him closer. Time lost its meaning. The only truth in her universe was Jake.

Abruptly, he sat up with a soft curse, studied her a moment, and stroked one work-roughened thumb across her lower lip.

She shuddered at the pure electricity in his caress, powerless to do move or speak.

Without a word, he stood, set his hat on his head, and left. A moment later the screen door slammed.

Annie touched her lips, trying to recapture the feel of Jake's fire. Why had he left? What secret barrier kept Jake from making love to her? Or was he wiser than she?

Chapter Six

"Annie," Jake muttered, stroking Bandit's sweat-dampened neck. Four days had passed since he'd found her treed by Old Sin. He'd planned to give her hell for riding out alone. But when he'd thought of her and the old boss cow, his only goal had been to get to her fast. The memory of her wedged against him in the saddle still sent a hot rush through his blood.

"Damn." He breathed deep, recalling the temptation of her body beneath him on the couch. It had taken all his resolve to pull away and leave. He still wanted to kiss her, taste her lips, and feel her hands stroke him.

Absently, he patted his stallion as he watched some young cattle drift toward the stream. Others stopped to graze. A few moved into the shade of the cottonwoods. They had food, water, and shelter. Too bad he couldn't solve his own problems as easily. Every six months taxes ate up more of his savings than these growing steers could eat in a week. Five years ago his dad had mortgaged the ranch to get equipment and cattle. Now Jake had to come up with a hefty payment every month to stay current. Old news, he mused, shifting in the saddle. What kept him awake at night was his cook.

Jake directed Bandit around a rocky outcrop to a spot overlooking the valley, and scanned the section of Rainbow Road ahead and below for Annie's car. She'd planned a trip to town after lunch. Why should he worry? He understood why. She wouldn't be the first to go down that road and never return.

Shaking his head at his own foolishness, he rode toward the ranch house.

Annie fingered the brim of the straw cowboy hat, adjusting the tilt. "Some fancy pot rustler," she said, grinning at her reflection in the old fashioned dresser mirror.

"Una cocinera muy bonita," came Jake's soft drawl from the open doorway.

"What?" Annie faced him, her pulse beating double-time at his sudden appearance. Half a week had passed since the kiss, but the memory hummed between them.

"One very pretty cook." He stepped into the room, filling it with his male presence. His leather chaps and dirt-streaked clothes showed he'd just come in from riding the range. Sweat-dampened, his russet hair had fallen into waves, one strand curling across his broad forehead. Tired lines grooved deeper around his mouth and eyes.

"See you and Mamie got acquainted." He nodded to the shopping bag labeled Mamie's Boutique.

"She's nice." Annie took off her new hat and set it on the bed beside the bag. "It's only the middle of May and I needed this for protection from the sun. Mamie had a bunch of hats, so I got a bargain."

"Don't have to convince me." His spurs jingled as he moved closer—bringing the scents of outdoors and honest work. "Don't go riding without me or one of the hands with you."

"Are we back to that? If I have to, I'll saddle Sage and go out again."

"You're still a tenderfoot. Anything can happen. You could get lost and stuck after dark with coyotes on the prowl. A bull might charge you. Your horse could get spooked by a rattle-snake and throw you."

"And Elvis might abduct me."

"Dammit, Annie. It's not a joke."

"That's right. Being told what I can and can't do in an emergency or on my own time isn't funny."

She considered the stubborn set to his jaw. "Listen, Jake. I know you look at me and think, *city girl*. What you don't understand is that I've been taking care of myself and my sister, Gabbie, since I was eight. Our mother moved us dozens of times, trying to find work that paid a decent wage. We lived in everything from two rooms with hot plate and bathroom-down-the-hall hotels, to a small house with an honest-to-God garden." Annie smiled reminiscently. "The house was best. A retired train engineer next door taught me how to dig and plant my first garden.

Jake looked down at her through dark brown lashes. "I got the message. You're tough."

He offered her a cage of grasses. "Brought this for you."

"A surprise! I love surprises! Does it bite?"

His chuckle vibrated to her toes. "Depends on what you mean by 'bite.'"

Intrigued, she opened it. Nestled in a cushion of damp grass lay a small plant with an unopened bud, its roots still wrapped in a ball of earth.

"Jake." She pushed aside a leaf to show thorns on a dark green stem. "It's a rose. Where'd you get it?"

"Wild Rose Canyon. Elspeth and Jacob Stone settled there first. Great-grandma planted roses beside their cabin. Grandpa called it a sweetbrier rose. Even the leaves smell good."

Annie bent her head to sniff at the foliage. "Reminds me of apples."

Impulsively she stood on tiptoe and kissed his cheek. "Thank you, boss."

Clasping her shoulders, he slowly bent his head.

She swayed toward him, watching his eyes darken, anticipating the heat of his lips against hers.

With an abrupt motion, he dropped his hands, gazed at her with a grim twist to his lips, and strode to the door. Without looking back, he left, his passage down the hall marked by the faint jingle of spurs.

Three hours later, supper finished, Annie washed the dishes still wondering why Jake had stopped the kiss and left her as if running from the devil. Probably just as well. She didn't dare fall in love with him.

To distract herself, she planned meals for the next four days. Deep in thought, she was startled by a sound at the door and swung around as Travis stepped through from the dining area.

"Man, you just clipped ten years off my life."

"Didn't mean to spook you," he said, a smile lurking around his lips. "Here's your mail."

"Thanks." She wiped her hands and took the letters.

Travis grinned, scooped up an apple croissant cooling on the wire rack, and winked. "A growing boy needs sugar," he said, and left.

The return address on one letter puzzled her. *Regency Enterprises*. What did they want?

The late morning sun promised a hot afternoon as Jake strode up the path toward the house. He detoured to the garden at the south corner of the porch where Annie had planted the brier rose. Would this thorny shrub be the only thing left of Annie at the end of four months?

He realized that he would miss her, and the idea of her leaving was something he didn't want to think about.

He followed the aroma of baked bread into the kitchen, where she sat reading a letter.

"Taking a breather?"

She raised a too-bright smile toward him, and jammed a letter in her pocket. "A short one. Bread's finished. Kitchen's clean."

He took a step closer. Her eyes were shadowed.

"Problem?"

"No. Just something to think about."

Her expression eased. She bounced to her feet. "Come on. I can use your muscles to move a trunk in the attic."

A dozen chores waited for him, but he followed her up the stairs, admiring her long legs and nicely rounded bottom.

"I came up here yesterday searching for a picture to go over your mantel in the living room."

"Use what's here any way you want." He followed Annie into the small room under the steeply slanted roof, flooded by memories. The last time he'd come up here, five years earlier, had been at Stephanie's request to store the large portrait of his grandparents with their five children. The May heat had raised the temperature in the cramped room that morning, too. Now he smelled the same odors of dust and mothballs, and felt the familiar trickle of perspiration between his shoulder blades.

"This is the trunk I want moved," Annie announced. "The small table behind it matches the porch furniture."

She reminded him of a kid gone treasure hunting. One cheek sported a dusty smudge. Her bright hair curled around her vivid face, and her eyes sparkled like the deep blue of a springtime sky. God, she made him feel old and jaded.

"Out of the way," he said as she shoved against the old, metal-bound trunk. "That thing weighs as much as you."

"That's it." Annie darted into the narrow space and touched the table. "Haul this down to the porch, please."

He straightened and settled his thumbs in his back pockets. "That'll teach me to come into your kitchen."

He watched her pivot slowly, examining the clutter of boxes, old furniture, and even a dressmaker's dummy his mother had abandoned.

"Stuff's been here for years." He rested his palm on the trunk. "My great-grandfather brought this from Boston with his young bride. She hated this place at first, but she stayed with him. Stuck it out. Didn't cut and run."

Annie laid one hand on his sleeve. His arm twitched with the suppressed urge to pull her closer.

"Jake," her voice sounded wistful. "I'm jealous. You know your family's history. You have things you can touch and say, 'This belonged to my grandmother, my great-grandfather.' " Her fingers tightened. "We moved so much the only thing I have to remember Grandma by is one faded photograph."

He looked down into her eyes. Misted with memories, they had a dreamy, yearning look.

The rattle of the ranch truck broke the tenuous spell. He emptied his lungs. "Buck's back with the coupling for the pump."

Jake hoisted the table. Her words followed him down the steps. "Put it beside the porch chair where Travis smokes."

Jake paused to open the outside door. Was she making a play for Travis? Shrugging, he told himself it didn't matter as long as she did her job. Just one more reason not to get involved.

Annie heard the door close. For a few minutes she'd felt a shared closeness with Jake. Idly, she stroked the carved nose of a rocking horse and set it in motion. Even out of the house, Jake dominated this room filled with the stored dreams of the Stone family.

She sat and thought and wished for the deep roots Jake had here.

An hour later, she'd hung the large portrait over the fireplace mantel, and scattered items from the attic around the living room.

That afternoon, she saw Jake heading toward the ranch truck, grabbed her wallet, and raced out to join him.

"I'm going into town with you," she said, snapping the seat belt.

"Got a business appointment." He started the engine and swung onto the road. "You'll have an hour to kill."

Annie shrugged. "That's easy. When I'm finished, I'll get a cup of coffee and see Verna."

They drove in silence until they came to Gold Creek, where clear water curled and rippled around huge red boulders. "Those chunks of sandstone came a long ways."

"Miles." Jake turned onto the narrow, wooden bridge. His voice carried above the rumble of tires on the thick boards. "Water comes down the creek in a red flood when it rains heavy."

They jounced over the short, graveled stretch and onto the paved road toward Dripping Springs.

"In August we get monsoon rains. Every dip and low spot

can flood. You don't ever want to get caught in a real gulley-washer.''

A chill raced down Annie's spine. "I'll remember. In L.A. and Orange counties we got enough rain to flood the streets. One time my car stalled and started to float.''

"I saw that when we lived there. Storm drains got clogged.''

"Hey, maybe we were neighbors and didn't know it,'' she said. "Where did you live?''

His shoulders tensed. He gripped the steering wheel hard enough to make his knuckles whiten. "My . . . wife and I lived near Park La Brea off Wilshire Boulevard. She loved it there. Always going somewhere, shopping, lunch with friends, museums, theaters, parties, nightclubs.''

Annie smiled at him. "Don't you miss it?''

"No. She did." He raked her with a swift glance. "How about you?''

"I'd like to see my friends again.'' Fond memories surfaced, Beth, Darryl, elderly Mrs. Nguyen, and her other neighbors at the residential motel.

"Men?''

"Not the way you mean it.'' Blindly, she faced the side window. Was he jealous? She couldn't let her attraction to Jake grow. He was struggling to keep his ranch. All her life she'd lived on the thin edge, one step above poverty. One wrong move would threaten her security again.

The car swooped down and up a dip in the road. The quick movement left her memories behind. Gathering her scattered thoughts, she reminded herself that her mother's struggle to feed and clothe her and her sister was in the past. The letter from Regency Enterprises pointed to a future.

He turned the corner onto Main Street. "Going to Mamie's? I'll part there and walk to the bank.''

"Any place'll do.''

They passed a strutting, potbellied man in a beige uniform with a big brass star on his pocket. Jake slowed the car. "I better take it easy,'' he said. "That's the sheriff, Sam Morgan. He'd love to throw me in the *juzgado*.''

"What's a huz-god-oh?''

"Jail. Also known as the hoosegow, which is the English version. Morgan's fair, but he's an ex-Texas Ranger and hard-nosed as they come."

Jake parked the car. "His hands were charged with drunk and disorderly once. The judge released them to me over Sam's objections. I set them to digging postholes and stringing wire." His eyes gleamed. "They'll think a helluva a lot more than twice before they cause any trouble again in town."

Annie opened the door before he could reach it and met Jake on the wood plank sidewalk. "I'll see you at the cafe when you're finished."

"Got it." He paused, brushed a tendril of hair away from her cheek. "I'm meeting Cliff Wallis at the bank. Wish me luck." With that, he tugged on the brim of his hat and strode toward the brick and concrete building.

Whispering "Good luck," she watched him disappear through the heavy glass doors.

An hour later she sat in a booth at the Coffee Cup Cafe facing the entrance, and sipped a glass of iced tea.

Jake walked in and stood at the door. He took off his hat and held it.

Verna called, "The usual, Jake?"

"Some other time. I want to get home." He held the door for Annie.

In a few minutes, they were headed out of town. Annie saw the tension in Jake's shoulders and the set of his jaw. She stayed quiet, hoping he'd tell her what was wrong. His grim expression stalled any questions.

By time they'd rattled across the creek bridge onto Rainbow Valley land, Annie asked, "What's bothering you, Jake?"

He eyed her, shrugged, and parked in the shade cast by a thick grove of cottonwoods. They got out of the truck and wordlessly he took her arm. They threaded through the trees to the banks of Gold Creek. A hot, resin-scented breeze swept down from the distant desert land and rustled through the bright green leaves. Water chuckled between the red banks ahead.

Jake picked up a handful of stones. Methodically he tossed them—one by one—into the swift-moving creek.

"Russell wants to buy the mortgage on my ranch."

Annie's breath caught in her throat. The idea sickened her. "Can he do that? Is it legal?"

Jake's face hardened. "If he comes up with enough money, and the bank officers agree, he can."

"The ranch belongs to you." She snatched up a thin, broken branch with two leaves clinging to it, and waved it in his face. "Your family settled this land. Russell doesn't belong on Rainbow land."

"Whoa." Jake threw up one hand to protect his face. "Don't get all lathered up."

"I'm not." She lowered the branch. "Well, maybe a little." Concentrating on the raised veins on one leaf, she asked, "What would happen if he did buy it?"

"Nothing, as long as I make the payments on time." He threw a larger rock into the creek. "Trouble is, Wallis turned down my request for a loan. I need the money to hire more help and expand my operation, or I'll get behind in my payments." His tone sounded neutral, controlled, but Annie saw his fist tighten around the last few stones.

She dropped the leafy twig and rested her hand on his taut fingers. "Jake, don't get in a stew. Isn't grazing good this year?" She pried at his fingers. "Besides, squeezing those rocks to dust won't help the calves grow any faster."

Through her sensitive fingertips, she felt the tension lessen in his knuckles and tendons. Finally, he opened his hand and dropped the last few pebbles. Dents and dark red patches in his hard palm marked the places where stone had met tough flesh.

He brushed the dust off his hands, wiped them on his jeans, and rested his arm on her shoulder with his fingers gently brushing the nape of her neck.

Reaching up, she touched his sleeve. "What are you thinking?"

He met her eyes, then looked away. "It all comes down to money."

She licked her lips, searching for a way to broach her idea.

"How about taking on a few paying guests at Rainbow? You've got three cottages and an empty bunkhouse going to waste."

"Dudes?" Jake snapped around, facing her. "Hell, no! I don't have time to entertain a bunch of greenhorns."

"Make it a *working* guest ranch. They're popular now. Big bucks in it. One of my classmates got a job at the Flying C in Colorado. She loves it."

Annie paused for Jake's response. All she got was grim silence. Drawing in a quick breath, she continued. "You and the guys grumble about needing more cowhands. You could work the dudes into a sweat, and they'd think you were doing them a favor."

"Finished?" he asked in a deceptively soft voice.

"Nope. Assign two or three guests to each of your men. Let them move the cattle to new grazing like you discussed at dinner last night." She hesitated at his tight-jawed expression, then plunged ahead. "And write you a check for the privilege."

Jake leaned one shoulder against a nearby tree and folded his arms, his expression still closed. The hot desert wind ruffled his auburn hair. It did nothing to soften the chill in his voice. "Damn, you're as determined as a cutting horse with a calf on the line. Have you looked at the empty buildings real close? The cottages need reshingling. I'd have to upgrade the bunkhouse, add new bathrooms, and divide it into rooms."

"So you've already considered the idea."

"Not me. Stephanie wanted the ranch sold to some hot-shot developer. They had it all worked out, thought I'd cave in and sell." He levered away from the tree and moved toward her. "Stay out of my business."

She raised her chin a combative inch. "I'm *not* Stephanie. I'm only trying to help you keep your ranch."

"Save it for some poor sap who wants a laugh."

Annie braced her hands on her hips and glared at him. "Or for someone who's not too proud to know what's good for him and his ranch."

Chapter Seven

"May thirtieth," Jake muttered, wondering how the month had slipped away. Draining his after-dinner coffee, he set the mug on the small table and leaned back in the porch chair.

As he watched Steve—in the glare of the yard light—load his rodeo rig into the truck bed, he thought about the last two weeks. Since Wallis had turned down the loan application, the hands had each done the work of ten men, moving cattle, mending fences, and culling dry cows and rank ones for the beef pen. Even Annie had pitched in to help vaccinate, loading a syringe for each calf after they'd branded it.

The screen door closed. "Want more coffee?"

Jake held out his mug. Annie worked hard and didn't complain, he thought as he watched her fill the mug. Unlike Stephanie, Annie was always up at dawn, cooking and cleaning. She fit in with the men and had made a place for herself. The ranch house hadn't run this well in years.

"You've done enough. Leave the pot and sit a spell."

Instead of dropping into the chair, she perched on the porch with her feet on the top step. "Is Steve taking a horse to ride in the Memorial Day rodeo?"

Jake joined her, sitting close enough to brush hips and elbows.

He heard her soft, indrawn breath at the contact. "Doesn't need one. He'll ride saddle broncs in the two go-rounds."

"Like he does here?" She faced him, her eyes dark and mysterious in the starlight.

"Not exactly." Jake wondered if she knew how close he was to kissing her. So soft-looking, yet so strong. He touched a stray curl fluttering against her cheek in the cool desert breeze. "Steve'll use a special flat saddle, and the bronc will do its damndest to buck him off."

Annie looked away. "It sounds dangerous."

"No more than breaking green stock." He slid one arm around her waist, his fingers resting just under the curve of her breast, and felt her shiver. "Steve only has to stay on for eight seconds until the buzzer, then the pickup rider will get him."

She tipped her head back, gazing at the night sky. "I'm still worried, but don't tell Steve. He's so confident he'll win a hefty purse. He's got big plans for the money."

Leaning closer, Jake breathed in her fragrance. "Steve wants to buy a spread, and—I want to do this." He turned her toward him and set his lips on the tender pulse point at the base of her throat. Her delicate womanly scent set his blood pounding.

"Jake?" she whispered. Her slender fingers threaded through his hair as her breasts pressed against his chest.

A hot surge of desire flooded his body. "Annie," he muttered, and stroked a line of kisses up the curve of her neck and jaw to her lips. Her fingers trembled and spread across his scalp. Her breath quickened and he knew she wanted him with the same fire as he wanted her. Drawing her body tighter against his, he swept one hand down her spine to her hips.

Behind them, the screen door opened and Travis said, "Boss, I hate to break this up, but Tomás just lit out of the barn like his tail's on fire."

Jake muttered a raw oath and stood up. He heard Annie gasp, then chuckle.

Before reaching the lawn, the slim wrangler called, "Boss. It's Lady. Looks like *el potro* comes."

"She's foaling early?" With a leap, Jake cleared the other stairs. Travis joined him in a race to the barn. He didn't waste his breath swearing, but the sexual need of moments earlier intensified his temper. Lady was his prize chestnut cutting horse, bred to Bandit. Their foal would be the foundation of his new herd.

Annie followed the two men into the barn. A bare light bulb cast a glow down the center aisle. The air was filled with the warm scent of hay and horses. They passed other stalls, then stopped in front of the largest one.

The pregnant mare wandered around her box restlessly. From time to time, she kicked up a hind foot or swished her tail. Finally, she stood, head down, ripples apparent along her sides. Annie felt a pang at the sight.

She watched Jake quietly open the gate and go in. Slowly, he stepped through the deep bed of fresh straw to the trembling mare's side.

"Easy, girl," he soothed, rubbing her sweaty back and haunches. "I'll stay here."

Lady softly whickered, nosing at his hair.

Travis slipped in beside him. "Want me to spell you later?"

"Just toss me a jacket. I'll stick here until she foals."

"I'm not goin' anywhere." Travis moved to the mare's other side.

"That makes three of us," Annie said, watching from outside the stall.

"It's goin' to be a while," Jake said in a low drawl, stroking the mare's neck.

A horse whickered. Looking up the aisle, Annie saw Sage stick her nose over the top rail of a stall, and stare at her with soft brown eyes.

Annie felt drawn to the gentle buckskin. Hesitantly she moved closer, laid a hand on the patient mare's neck, then scratched the sensitive spot between the horse's ears.

Sage closed her eyes in apparent pleasure. Annie's tension eased. She smiled in delight. Her sense of dread around Sage had disappeared.

Across the aisle in another stall, the gelding, Big Red, thrust his nose over the wooden gate and quietly gazed at her.

Bouyed by new confidence, Annie patted the horse's neck. He relaxed under her touch, and her confidence soared.

She returned to the gate outside Lady's stall, and watched Jake with the laboring mare.

He spread another layer of clean straw, moving calmly around Lady. Next, he washed his hands and arms in a bucket of hot soapy water and antiseptic, then checked the mare's progress.

Toward dawn, at Jake's urging, Steve, Travis, and the other men left for the rodeo.

Annie stroked Lady's nose while Jake examined the mare again. "Looks like another hour will do it. Foal's in the right position."

"You're dead tired, Annie. Go to bed. I'll stay here."

She smothered a yawn. "I can go another hour or so. Why don't you crash while I babysit?" She patted the space beside her. "The straw's soft. We'll be here for Lady."

He dropped down beside her. "We'll both watch."

Annie scooted around behind him. "You're wound tighter than a broken pocket watch. I can fix that."

He felt her fingers kneading his shoulders. The rhythmic pressure and release slowly eased his taut muscles. Her hands felt damned good. For now, it was enough.

Jake reminded himself not to let down his guard. She'd be leaving, just like all the other women in his life had left.

The laboring chestnut settled down on her side in the deep bedding. Jake washed his hands in a fresh bucket of soapy water and antiseptic, and returned to the roomy stall.

Annie knelt beside the mare, stroking the white blaze on its nose. "Is she all right?"

"Looks normal to me."

Jake moved to the opposite side of Lady, deliberately putting more distance between himself and Annie.

"Something wrong, Jake?"

"No. Nothing."

Annie stared at him a moment. Bewilderment flickered in her eyes. She touched Lady's side, hesitated, then ran her hand over the chestnut's swollen belly.

A sunbeam lit the red in the mare's chestnut coat and haloed Annie's bright hair. Jake heard her whisper, "Good girl, brave little mama, we're proud of you."

The laboring horse shuddered and the last stage of birth began.

Annie scrambled back out of the way.

When the foal's forefeet and head appeared, Jake checked its position again. "Give her room, Annie."

He searched her expression for signs of queasiness. Instead, he saw her eyes fill with tender excitement. "Jake, this is wonderful. I see its front feet. It looks like it's diving into the world."

"Natural birth position. We'll let nature take its course."

The mare gave a final heave and the slippery foal lay on the straw. Jake stripped the wet membrane from its face. Lady pushed to her feet and started cleaning her newborn.

The baby struggled to a sitting position. Watching its strong movements, Jake felt deep satisfaction and excitement. This foal represented a new chance for Rainbow to grow.

"Jake, can I touch it?" Annie asked.

"Yeah, Lady's accepted you."

Annie went down on her knees in the thick straw, gently caressing its neck. "Is it a boy or a girl?"

"It's a filly." He gave her a soft cloth and began wiping the little chestnut's back with another one.

"A baby girl!" Annie kissed the top of the foal's head. "I love it." She dried the newborn, moving the cotton towel around delicate ears and nostrils, and across the miniature muzzle.

When Jake and Annie toweled off its coat, the foal gave a muffled squeak.

Lady whickered, sniffing at her baby.

"Give the little gal a chance to get up." Jake wished he had a camera to take a picture of Annie and the foal with Lady hovering over the two.

"Come on, the momma's getting nervous."

"Oh." Annie rose and moved back. "I can't believe it's so tiny. Look at the little hooves. They're perfect."

"Do tell," Jake said in wry amusement. He watched the foal waver to its feet, totter, lose its balance, and collapse in the straw bed, a startled expression on its face.

Annie crooned, "Poor baby. Keep trying." She glanced at Jake.

"That's a strong newborn," he reassured her.

"She's darling." Annie watched the little chestnut's wobbly steps as it instinctively searched for and found its first meal.

Jake leaned against the railing beside Annie in companionable silence. Morning sun warmed the barn and released the baled hay's sweet, fresh scent. Dust motes jittered in a sunbeam. In the corral outside, Bandit neighed.

While Jake cleared out the old straw and forked in a thick new layer, Annie filled the drinking bucket with fresh water.

He saw her smother a yawn. "Annie, get some sleep. We're all done here."

"Thanks, boss." She smiled at him, and patted Sage on the nose as she walked past the buckskin's stall.

With the foal busily nursing, Jake headed for a shower. He stood under the warm water and replayed the previous few hours. Rinsing off the soap, he recalled the first time Stephanie saw a foal born. She'd staggered away from the scene and upchucked her breakfast. After that, she'd avoided all the pastures during calving season, driving into Las Vegas or Los Angeles to stay for weeks.

Jake toweled himself dry and flopped on his bed. Annie had learned more about the ranch in the short time she'd been there than Stephanie had in their sad five years.

He stacked his hands behind his head and grinned at the sunlit ceiling, recalling Annie's excitement over the newborn foal. She'd pitched in to help as if she'd been on a ranch all her life.

"Like she'd lived on a ranch," he muttered. Annie had changed *his* ranch from a place to eat and run and fall into bed at night, to an inviting home. Dishes were done. The cookie jar was always filled. And the men crowded to the table like a herd of young stallions jostling each other for the choicest feed.

Thinking of Annie made him quiver like Bandit scenting a mare in heat. When he held her in his arms, touched her silky skin, breathed her sweet scent, he ached to make love.

Muttering a curse, he shifted to ease the press of the sheet against his arousal. It didn't help.

Jake slipped out of bed and walked to the window. His nude body cooled in the desert breeze rippling the curtains.

He gazed down at the barn and pasture drowsing in the morning sun.

It wasn't the first time Annie had been at his side. In the last weeks she'd doubled her work load, doing the house and meals, and helping with the cattle. She'd stayed with him while he groused about not getting the loan. She'd even come up with a plan to make a profit by taking in guests. Maybe he should take her suggestion seriously. Yet, the idea of wannabe cowboys stuck in his craw.

"Dudes." Jake braced his hands on the windowsill. He'd had his fill of guests at his mother's weekend parties when he was a kid. Mom had made it clear he was to keep out of the way of her friends, especially the men.

Fatigue drove him back to bed and into exhausted sleep.

He woke to bright sunshine, swearing at the clock face. Twelve o'clock and there were chores to be done.

As he opened the top dresser drawer, he caught sight of his grandmother's carved bone hummingbird comb. She'd worn it every day, tucked in her black hair where it swept back into a bun.

In a rush of pride over his heritage, he'd tried to give it to Stephanie soon after their marriage.

She'd laughed, and said, "How quaint. No, thanks. It's just not my style."

Impulsively, Jake tucked the carved comb into his shirt pocket.

He stamped into his boots, snapped his jeans on the way out the bedroom door, and buttoned his shirt on the stairway. The aroma of fresh-perked coffee greeted him, but the kitchen was empty. He poured himself a cup of the fragrant brew. So Annie had gone back to bed, and he couldn't begrudge her the rest.

Carrying the full cup, he walked to the barn and noted the horses' drinking trough filled with clear water, a new salt lick set in place, and fresh hay in the net. A full wheelbarrow sat outside the barn door ready to be dumped. He frowned, remembering he'd left it empty after cleaning the birthing stall. Who'd been here doing chores?

He found the answer inside the barn. Lady peacefully munched at a bucket of grain. Annie knelt in a bedding of clean straw, her eyes shining as she cuddled the filly.

"Jake, I left a surprise for you in the wheelbarrow."

He hunkered down beside Annie and the foal. "You've been busy. Thanks." He wanted to touch her face, kiss her. Find out if she tasted as good as she had last night. "Did you sleep?"

"Three hours. I couldn't wait to see the baby when I woke up."

The filly made a funny little squeak, and Lady lowered her head to sniff at her daughter.

Annie stood and walked outside the stall. Jake followed. Propping elbows on the top rail, they watched the mare and foal in companionable silence.

"Annie," Jake dipped his hand into his pocket and took out the comb. "This belonged to my grandmother. I want you to have it."

"Jake, it's beautiful." She cradled it in her hand and traced one carved wing raised in flight. "This is an heirloom. I shouldn't take it."

Gently, he clasped her hand, pressing the comb into her palm. "Grandma would've liked you. She worked hard on the ranch and took pride in making it comfortable for everyone here. So do you." He released her hand and curved his fingers over her slim shoulders. "Keep it and don't be afraid to wear it. Grandma did every day."

Annie swept her hair back from her face on one side and tucked the ornate comb into her bright curls. Standing on tiptoe, she kissed his cheek.

He slid his hands down to her waist, held her closer, and touched his lips to hers.

* * *

Annie waited outside the bunkhouse in the early afternoon. Jake saw the worry in her eyes.

"How's Steve doing? He looked awful pale."

"Touchy as a cow on the prod, but he's been dumped by other horses. He'll live. He sure won't be rodeoing for a while."

"Can I get something for him besides a little soup?" She moved closer and laid a hand on his arm.

He smoothed a strand of hair away from her face. "Save me some?"

Saddling Bandit, Jake rode out to find a small band of herd quitters in the north breaks. Once he located them, he'd chivvy them back to the main herd in the nearest pasture. With Steve out of action, they'd all have to double up on work.

He looked back toward the great rise of sandstone that marked his home. Annie's suggestion of opening a working guest ranch nagged him.

Bandit blew a gust of air. Jake patted the horse, swung into the saddle, and rode to an overlook. Here, above the floor of Rainbow Valley, he looked across the great sweep of land. How could he and his small crew do all the work without more help?

The real question was, could he bend to new ideas without breaking?

Quarter to eight, and no Jake. Annie stationed herself on the porch. Sunset colors were fading as the sun dipped lower in the west. What if his horse had stepped into a hole and thrown him? Apprehension made her mouth dry. Maybe a rattler had struck him and he was on the ground, in agony, fighting the deadly venom.

Should she ask Travis to search for Jake? No, Travis had gone to the bunkhouse to check on Steve, and she couldn't stand to wait any longer.

Annie hurried across the lawn, past the corral, and partway

down the trail, seeking any sign of Jake in the darkening valley. If she didn't see him, she'd saddle Sage and try to find him.

An evening breeze moaned through the trees. The shade she'd welcomed in daytime heat made the trail gloomy in the waning dusk. Even the birds were quiet, except for one long call of an owl that raised the hair on the back of her neck.

As she started uphill toward the barn, she heard the distant steady thud of a horse's hooves. Jake rode Bandit around a curve in the trail and reined to a stop beside her.

"Lose something, Annie?"

"My patience, waiting for you to come and eat." She moved closer, swallowing her fear of Bandit, and put her hand on the stirrup strap. Jake's clothes and hat were caked with dust. Deep shadows obscured his face. He looked bone-tired. "Jake Stone, you don't have the sense of a turkey in the rain to work yourself like this."

He edged Bandit away from her. "Forget the lecture. I'll do what's necessary to keep this outfit going."

He kneed his horse into a walk and headed toward the barn. Glaring at his back, she shouted, "Dinner in ten minutes." He didn't respond.

"Jerk," she muttered, trudging up the dirt track. But deep inside she felt the coiled tension ease. He'd come back safe.

Full dark had fallen by the time Jake joined her in the kitchen. Wet hair, clean jeans, and a shirt told her he'd showered. He slumped into a chair at the small table and stared at the food she set in front of him.

"Don't expect it to dance, Jake. Eat before I feed it to the coyotes."

"Bossy," he muttered, cutting a section of roast pork.

"In the kitchen I am." She poured his coffee and went back to kneading dough in a large crockery bowl.

Travis joined them, refilled his coffee mug, and lolled in the chair across from Jake. "Boss, you look like somethin' a self-respectin' buzzard would reject."

Jake ate a chunk of bread, and gave his top hand a thin smile. "I'll live. How's Steve?"

"Ready to chew nails. He had top score, an eighty-one after

the first go-round. Could've been high scorer for the day if the damn bronco hadn't kicked Charlie Smitt's horse.''

"So that's what happened. Charlie's a good pick-up rider.''

Annie draped a clean dishtowel over the first batch of dough and started on the second. "Poor Steve. He didn't win the money and he's stuck with medical bills.''

"The kid bought rodeo insurance,'' Jake said. "It'll cover most of the cost.''

He finished his meal and pushed back from the table. "Thanks for dinner. I'll be in my office. Travis, I have something to show you.''

Both men left.

Annie thought back to the letter she'd received from Regency Enterprises. They were considering her for the kind of job she'd hoped for. One offering her the money she needed to at last feel secure . . . and the prestige she felt she'd earned.

It was what she wanted. Wasn't it?

Verna rode past the ranch house the next afternoon, and looped the reins of her roan horse on the corral fence.

Annie ran out to greet her.

Smiling, the dark-haired woman took off her riding gloves and stuffed them in her jeans pocket. "Annie, you're lookin' mighty fine. Jake treatin' you good?''

"All the guys here are great.'' Annie preceded the older woman up the porch steps and opened the door. "I've got biscotti and cranberry cookies cooling. Can you stay long enough for coffee?''

"Best deal I've had today.'' She gestured at the kitchen. "You've done wonders here, honey. The place shines.''

"Thanks.'' Annie took a moment to look around the kitchen that had become a second home to her. Boy, would she miss this place if she went to Regency. She joined Verna with two cups of coffee and a plate of cookies.

Verna sampled the biscotti. "You're a dab hand with baking, Annie.''

"A what?''

"Expert." Verna finished the pastry. "You coming to the church Moonlight Picnic tomorrow evening? Ask Jake to bring you. If he won't, come by yourself. Most of the gals'll wear a summer skirt and blouse or dress. Bring enough rolls and salad for ten people."

"It sounds like fun. I'll see what Jake says."

After they talked about other local news, Verna said, "If you can find time to ride horseback, there's a lot more to see."

"I have. Buck keeps promising to take me to Wild Rose Canyon."

Verna chuckled. "Old coot ask you to marry him yet?"

"First night I was here." Annie grinned back. "Didn't seem too crushed when I said no."

"He's been asking me for years." Verna wrinkled her nose, but Annie thought she seemed a little wistful. "Maybe I'll surprise him one day and say yes. That'll knock the wind out of his gut."

Verna munched on a cookie, her expression growing more serious. "Jake's the one who needs a decent woman."

"That creep Russell talks about the subject as if he knew everything about it."

"Ben Russell." Verna's mouth twisted in disgust. "Him and Stephanie were an item until she decided Jake could give her a better deal, even bragged about it to me. Their marriage didn't stop Randy Russell. He'd go sneakin' behind Jake's back after the wedding, still sniffin' around Stephanie. Until the day she died, just about."

"I can't see any woman choosing Russell over Jake." Annie traced the rim of her cup, aching for Jake, for the betrayal he'd suffered from his wife, for what her death must have cost him. She heard enough from the people who understood him to know not to bring up the subject of Stephanie.

"There ain't no figurin' some people." The older woman stood. "Time to hit the road."

Annie pressed a bag of cookies in Verna's hands, and they strolled onto the porch as Jake rode into view. "Here comes the boss now."

Jake looped Big Red's reins to the corral fence before walking toward the house stripping off his work gloves.

Verna said, "Howdy, Jake. I was just telling Annie she's done wonders with the house and yard."

"She sure has."

Frowning, Verna glanced at Annie. "Jake Stone, you ought to be ashamed of yourself. Annie works herself into a frazzle cooking and making the place look nice. And you can't say more than that?"

He set one booted foot on the bottom step and tipped back his hat. "You got me there."

"That's right." Verna said. "She needs a break. I told her about the Moonlight Picnic tomorrow. Why don't you drive her there? Pastor Wayne's expecting you to help with the kids' races like last year."

He slapped the gloves, bundled in one hand, against his thigh. "Don't have time. I've got a ranch to run."

Verna touched Annie's arm. "Honey, you better catch a ride with Buck."

Jake went past them toward the door. "Moonlight picnic," he muttered. "Just what I need with a hand laid up."

"I'll be on my way." Verna patted Annie's shoulder and led her to the corral fence. "Don't pay him no mind. Sometimes he spouts off before he thinks. I'll see you tomorrow evening."

Forget Jake Stone, Annie thought, marching back into the house. She'd go with Buck.

Jake heard the screen door slam as he double-checked Lady and her foal. He wondered just what the hell was wrong with him. Maybe it had been too long since he'd been on a moonlit picnic.

The next afternoon, Jake found Annie in the kitchen mixing diced apples, celery, walnuts, raisins, and mayonnaise in a large bowl. "That for the picnic?"

"My version of a Waldorf salad. I've figured a way to keep it chilled until it's served." She covered with bowl with foil, storing it in the refrigerator. "Your meal will be ready before

I leave. Monica's coming for Steve. The other guys said you gave them the night off.''

"They threatened to hogtie me if I didn't.''

The apron covering her shorts and sleeveless top only hinted at the curves underneath. Another step and the nerve ends in his skin registered her body's presence. He closed one hand around the top edge of the kitchen chair to keep from fingering the bright curls plastered to her damp forehead. He had a sudden image of her stretched out naked on his white sheets, her skin moist with passion. Jake licked his lips, remembering the taste of hers. They'd only kissed a few times, and he'd never seen her without clothes, but he could dream.

She glanced up at him, her eyes deep blue with awareness. "I'll save a helping of the salad and three rolls to go with your meal, Jake.''

Annie moved to the far end of the table and packed rolls for the picnic. "Buck says we should leave at six to get there in time. Your food will be on the table at ten to six and your dessert in the fridge.''

Clearing his throat, Jake said, "Pastor Wayne telephoned me last night. I can't disappoint the kids. Will you go with me instead of Buck?''

"I promised Buck first.'' She walked past him to the door and paused. "See you there.''

Not too surprised, Jake watched the door close behind her. He couldn't blame her for being mad after the way he'd blown up yesterday. Still, it was the first time he'd ever been turned down by a woman in favor of an old guy like Buck.

"Hell,'' he grumbled.

Chapter Eight

Jake remembered Stephanie at one Moonlight Picnic. Wearing a tight, short skirt and skimpy tank top, she'd snubbed the women and flirted with his friends. She'd complained to him about the food, and the kids shouting and chasing each other.

But Annie, now. Annie belonged here. She talked and laughed with everybody. Dressed in a bright, flowered skirt and ruffled white blouse, she looked cool and feminine.

By the time they'd finished eating and sampled the homemade ice cream, night had fallen. A cool, fragrant desert breeze set the colored lamps dancing.

Across the expanse of night-dewed grass, banjos, fiddles, and guitars tuned up. A single harmonica spun a lonely spell. Annie watched two men and a handful of teens set out chairs along the edge of the basketball court.

Jake wrapped his arm around her waist. "Want to dance first or go on a hayride?"

Annie wanted this day to last forever. "I've never been on a hayride."

"Suits me." He hugged her closer as they followed Verna and Buck to a wagon filled with summer-fresh hay. Half a dozen other couples had staked out spots. Jake found an empty corner at the rear opening, where he spread a blanket. He handed her onto the thick fabric, and stretched out beside her. "C'mere, Annie."

Annie snuggled into the circle of Jake's arms, absorbing the brilliance of stars poured across the night sky, the soft *clop* of horses' hooves, and the wonder of his tenderness. She sent up a silent prayer to make it last.

"Comfortable?" Jake's voice resonated against her back. He nuzzled the side of her neck, his breath stirring her hair. *"Un centavo* for your thoughts."

Kiss me. But she wouldn't say it aloud. Annie stroked his arm where it nestled across her waist. His hand moved higher, under her breasts, and she gasped.

She stilled his hand, gripping his strong wrist.

He loosened his hold, and she searched for a way to change the subject. "When was your first hayride?"

"Grandpa took me and some friends on my sixth birthday. 'Course we spent the time hollering like cowboys, throwing dried grass at each other, and wrestling."

Softly, she curled her fingers around his wrist, lulled by the warmth of his strong body. "You loved your grandparents, didn't you?"

"They lived in the foreman's cottage. My earliest memories are of toddling over there. Grandma always opened the cookie jar for me. When it was time to go, Grandpa'd hoist me onto his shoulders and take me home."

"Didn't your mother worry?"

"Naw. Usually, she didn't notice I was gone."

"She didn't miss—?"

His warm lips brushed Annie's cheek. "Spend time with your grandparents?"

"Don't I wish." Wondering why he'd cut off her question, she closed her eyes to capture the feel of his solid strength. "Mom and Dad moved a lot, always chasing one of his dreams. We traveled even more after he left, going from town to town for work. It was hard to keep up with mail."

He stroked the nape of her neck with warm fingers. "Pretty rough to move around so much."

"When it's all you know . . . " She looked over her shoulder at his shadowed face and gave him a faint smile. A light breeze stirred his hair. One of the horses snorted, and its harness jingled. Tucked in the intimacy of his arms and hidden by the night, she felt cocooned from the world, safe, secure. "I loved seeing new places. I'd plaster my face against the side window and look at the passing scenery. Mom would play the radio and we'd sing along. Sometimes, when we drove late, a station would fade or sign off. Then it would be just Mom, Gabbie, and me driving through the night."

"Poor kids," he said softly.

"Hey, don't feel sorry for us. My sister and I learned to stand on our own because Mom worked hard, long hours."

The wagon lurched. Jake's hold tightened. He stroked her shoulder, his fingers tantalizing the bare skin about her ruffle. She looked up at the night sky.

"The stars . . . they're so clear."

He chuckled. "It's the desert air. When I was a kid, my grandpa and I'd walk down to the corral and look at the sky. He'd point out the constellations and tell me their stories. My favorite was Orion."

Annie smiled. "One night a neighbor let me look at Jupiter through his telescope. I loved the bands of red and orange swirling around the planet, and its moons strung out like pearls against a black velvet sky. I wanted to fly there, to walk on strange lands, to find an untouched spot of my own."

His hand paused. "And have you found that place?"

"Not yet." She sighed. It was so easy to tell him things she'd never said to any other person, easy to reveal herself. She was afraid she was falling in love with Jake Stone.

Crickets chirped in the cool air. Whispers and low laughter drifted above the sounds of horses's hooves and the creak and groan of the wagon. The sweetly spiced scents of hay and desert plants hovered on the breeze.

Behind them, Buck murmured something and Verna chuckled.

A harmonica played snatches of "When You Wish Upon A

Star.'' Jake shifted her in his arms so she could look up into his moon-silvered eyes. ''Ever wish on a star?''

She nodded.

''Right before my junior high graduation prom. I wanted blue-eyed blond George Van Meer to take me.'' She smiled to cover the pain. ''When he did, I was over the moon. I walked around with stars in my eyes for two weeks.''

Jake touched his lips to her temple. ''George get roses for your corsage?''

''I don't know.'' She laughed against the bitter memory. ''I never went. No flowers. No dance. No graduation. Mom lost her job the night before the prom, and we moved early the next morning.''

She felt his lips press the top of her head.

''It was a good lesson. It taught me not to depend on other people to make me happy.''

''And you don't want anyone feeling sorry for you.''

Annie hated self-pity. She grinned at Jake. ''That's enough about me.''

The harmonica player had changed to ''Blue Moon.''

Wordlessly, Jake lowered his head and outlined the rim of her ear with his moist tongue. She shivered at the delicious warmth, and suddenly recalled other times he'd held her and then pushed her away.

With one finger, he tilted her face, but she turned her head and his lips only met the corner of her mouth.

She pulled away from him. ''I'm not ready for this,'' she said in a ragged breath.

Bewildered by her quick switch of mood, Jake let his arm and hand slide down to his lap. In the wash of moonlight, he saw her tight, trembling lips. ''Annie? What's going on?''

She moved back farther in the thick hay until she was braced against the wagon side. ''I should ask you the same thing. One minute you're friendly, the next you're acting like a jerk.'' Her voice was strained.

''I made some mistakes. So sue me. I still want you here with me.''

''Jake Stone—''

The roar of approaching trucks drowned out her words. What idiots were crowding the hayride on this narrow trail?

Tires spitting dirt, a white truck screamed up behind the wagon, swerved around, and moved parallel with it. The driver stuck his head out the open window and yelled, "Yee-haw!"

"What the hell?" Jake stood, and watched in disgust as Ben lay on the gas, made a wide loop around the front of the wagon, and came back. "It's Ben Russell. Drunk as a skunk."

He glanced at Annie. "Hang on. Horses might spook."

Another truck, with three cowhands riding in the open bed, blocked the road in front.

"Hey, get outta here," the driver shouted. "Yer scarin' the horses."

Raucous laughter greeted his command. A bottle sailed out of the window and shattered against the wagon.

Cursing, the teamster reined in the horses.

The truck's driver shouted, "We're stagin' a holdup, like the old days."

A woman passenger gasped. Another let out a low cry. Two of the men in the wagon got to their feet.

Jake looked at Annie again. She said, "I'm cool," and gave him a faint smile.

He waggled a hand at the other men, knowing they had women to protect. "I'll take care of this. It's between Russell and me."

Ben hauled himself up on the back of the wagon. "Came for my date." He leered at Annie.

She looked at the drunken rancher as if she'd smelled something rotten, Jake observed.

He stepped between her and Ben. "Russell, you're stinkin' drunk. Go home and sleep it off."

Weaving, the burly rancher grabbed the wooden rail. "Jus' feelin' good." He thrust his chin forward. "Get outta my way, Stone."

"Come on, Ben. I don't fight drunks. Call off your men and head on out."

"Who shays—says I'm drunk?" He peered at Annie. "You think I'm drunk, sweet thing?"

"Last chance, Russell." Jake didn't want Annie harassed, but he sure as hell didn't want her in the middle of a brawl.

Ben rubbed his eyes, swaying against the wood slats. "Yeah. Mebbe I am. Guess I'll go home," he mumbled. "Give me a hand, Stone."

"You got it." He held out his hand.

Lurching around him, Russell fell on his knees beside Annie. "You're givin' it to Jake. Gimme some, too." He pawed her, tried to kiss her.

With a cry, she shrank back.

Cursing, Jake reached past her and fastened his fist in Ben's shirt. "Apologize to the lady."

"Hell, no." Ben threw a punch. Jake turned to catch the blow on his shoulder, shielding her.

Annie didn't know what to do. Wedged between the two men, she couldn't move out of the way.

"Here, you rattlesnake, hit the road." Buck wrapped an arm around Cutter's head, but one of Ben's gang of rowdy cowhands yanked at Buck and pushed him out of the wagon.

"Buck!" Verna screamed, climbing over the side. She scrambled down and ran to where Buck had propped himself up on one arm. Her shadow, cast by the bright moon, melted into his while she wiped his face with the edge of her skirt.

In the meantime, Jake fought the four men. Blows and grunts, the thud of fists smacking into flesh marked the battle. The other men and women jumped or climbed from the wagon. Straw flew, adding to the confusing darkness.

Annie jerked off a shoe and hit whoever came into range, while avoiding Jake.

"Annie, get off the wagon," Jake panted. "Stay out of this."

"In your dreams." She whacked the tall man called Spade on his cheek and elbow.

He snarled an ugly word and shook her. Jake plucked him off, half-twisted to avoid Ben's fist, and fell beside Annie.

"Jake, Jake!" Scrambling to her knees, she tunneled through the crackly dried alfalfa and grass to find Jake, sneezing in the flying dust.

Spade grabbed a handful of her blouse, growling, "Outta

my way, bitch.'' Annie heard her blouse rip just as Jake exploded from the hay, carrying Spade back against the high sideboards.

Arms wrapped around her from behind. Annie reared backward to shake loose. Travis's familiar voice said, ''Give the boss room to fight,'' as he pulled her off the wagon.

''Help him.'' She flailed, trying to get away, but Verna grabbed her arm.

''Stay here, Annie. Jake'll do better if he knows you're out of the way.''

She saw Jake heave Spade out of the wagon, then turn and punch a second man. ''You're right. Damn. He's good.''

Travis vaulted into the wagon bed and took on a rough-looking cowboy. In the harsh shadows and pale light, men struggled and fell, cursed and grunted. Annie chewed her lip, trying to follow Jake's weaving form in the clouds of flying hay.

Someone yelled, ''Sheriff's coming.''

''Uh, oh,'' Buck muttered. ''Jake's in fer it now. Sam'd love to toss him into jail.''

Annie ran to the wagon. ''Jake, c'mon. Time to go home.''

He faced her, wiping his mouth with the back of his hand. Moonlight gleamed across his battered face. She stifled a grown. ''Get down. The fight's over. Sheriff Morgan's coming.''

''We're done here,'' Travis added, casually shoving back a limp fighter.

Jake looked down at Ben sprawled over a pile of hay. ''Be right there.'' He wrapped his fist in Russell's torn shirt and pulled him to a sitting position. ''You still owe Miss Reed an apology.''

Sullenly, the whipped man growled, ''Sorry.''

Jake bent closer to Russell. ''If I see you near her again, you'll end up carrying your teeth, not wearing them. Got it?''

''Yeah, I got it,'' he blubbered between cut lips.

Jake vaulted out of the wagon and winced when he landed. ''Nothin' like a good brawl,'' he said, obviously trying to downplay the fight.

She tugged him toward the safety of inky shadows under

the trees. "Come on," she said in a low voice. "Let's go home before the big, bad sheriff sees you."

"You okay?" Jake steadied her when she tripped over a branch. They went a few steps farther before Jake stumbled into a tree. Annie tucked an arm around his waist, offering her support.

"Thanks," he muttered. "Damned eye's swollen shut."

Together they walked along the edge of the road toward the parking lot. Through the trees, they saw Sam Morgan striding in the direction of the wagon, his powerful flashlight shining across the rough track.

At Jake's truck, Annie put out her hand for the keys.

Driving through the night toward Rainbow Valley, Annie remembered another night, a night when Jake had said no woman was worth fighting for. Now he slumped against the seat beside her, bruised, cut, his breath hissing through his lips each time they hit a bump.

He'd fought to protect her. Nobody had ever done that. Her throat clogged. Her eyes filled with hot tears. She wanted to stop and bathe his hurts with those tears; to hold him and kiss away the pain.

"Annie?" His fingers brushed her cheek. "Crying?"

"No," she lied. She would never admit to her own vulnerability. Not to Jake.

Chapter Nine

Jake woke with a groan. The picnic fight had left him as stiff as an old, bunged-up cowpuncher.

As usual, Annie had gotten up ahead of him and the other hands. Swearing at his bruised and swollen knuckles, he dressed.

The smell of fresh coffee and bacon sizzling on the griddle greeted him when he eased his aching body into place at the table. While he drank the large glass of orange juice, he ignored the way it stung his cut lip, remembering instead, Annie's kisses.

"My hero." Annie bounced a plateful of scrambled eggs, bacon, and fried potatoes in front of him, and returned a few seconds later with coffee and hot biscuits.

He put his fork down and cleared his throat, unsure of how to start. He vaguely remembered her patching him up before he'd drifted off to sleep, and how much he had liked her gentle ministrations.

Had he done anything that might've upset her somehow? She seemed distant—

Male voices and the thump of boots interrupted him. Annie said, "Crew's coming," and disappeared into the kitchen.

Jake swore under his breath.

Travis sauntered in, grinning. "Hell, boss, if I didn't know better, I'd say you got the business end of Old Sin."

Jake stared pointedly at Travis's swollen eye and bruised cheek. "If I did, you stood next in line."

Cheerfully, Travis dropped into his chair and gulped down the glassful of juice. "Yeah, got some of mine back for the night they jumped me at the Red Bull."

Buck hobbled to the table cursing Ben Russell and his gang of rowdies. He grabbed a biscuit, broke it open, and buttered it. "Fight last night warn't such a bad thing. Verna was right sweet about patching me up." He took a healthy bite of biscuit. "An' she damned near kissed my boots off."

Tomás and Steve joined them, grinning their thanks to Annie as she settled heaping platters of eggs, fried potatoes, bacon, and a basket of warm biscuits on the table.

Jake got a refill of coffee and turned to his ramrod. "Was Sheriff Morgan steaming lat night?"

"Hot enough to fry an egg." Travis piled food on his plate. "He took special exception to the news Russell insulted Annie and started a fight."

Buck chimed in. "By the time ol' Travis was done talkin', Sam had the handcuffs on Ben an' Spade. He said he was gonna hold 'em overnight until they sobered up. He warned them to stay away from Rainbow."

"Sam Morgan can be a decent sheriff." Jake silently welcomed Travis's news. He had too much to do to waste time in court.

He put down his cup and stood. "I'm going to check the windmill at Deadman's Creek pasture. Travis has the jobs for you."

Jake spent half the day wrestling with the broken pump shaft. At three o'clock, he spied Travis galloping toward the windmill. With a final twist, Jake set the machinery in motion and watched the sand-scoured blades revolve in the hot wind.

"Belly up to the bar, boys," Jake announced. "It's on me."

Thirsty cattle crowded around the edge of the metal tank as cold water once more gushed from the pipe.

Travis reined in his roan gelding. "See you got it running again."

"For now." Jake wiped his face, bone-tired. "The whole ranch is slowly falling apart. Between new regulations and the damned cattle prices, I don't have the money to fix things right."

Travis swung off his horse. "My offer's still good."

"I won't take your savings." Jake stared at the cattle. "Annie suggested a way to make the ranch pay by taking on working guests." He looked at Travis to assess his response. "Tomorrow I'll go in to Prescott to arrange financing. If I get it, I can do the renovations."

"We can use the extra help." Travis tipped his hat and grinned. "It'll be better 'n any rodeo, watchin' tenderfeet learn the ropes."

"Here's to rich greenhorns," Jake said, raising his thermos.

Late the next day, Jake crossed Gold Creek heading home. Now, with an added hundred thousand dollars in the ranch account to start and a generous line of credit, he could make improvements, including the road currently rattling his brains. He couldn't wait to tell Annie.

As he pulled into the yard and parked, he saw Annie and Steve at the meadow pasture watching Lady and her foal.

He opened the truck door and walked down the dirt path, frowning at the mended fences and run-down building. It would be a hell of a lot of work to fix everything up, but at lease now he could. It still didn't guarantee more than breaking even.

Steve's grin faded as he looked at Jake. "Annie brought a carrot to Lady. I followed."

"Jake, watch this." Annie stretched one hand, palm up, toward the mare and little filly. "Lady's baby likes me." The foal pranced toward them, its coat shining with red highlights in the bright afternoon sun. It snuffled at Annie's hand, lipped her palm, then danced away.

"Since you were midwife, want to name the foal?"

Annie beamed. "I know the perfect name—Sun Dancer."

"Sounds good. I'll register her with the name." He gave Steve a hard look. "Tack done?"

"Most of it." The young cowhand tipped his hat lower over his eyes. "I'll go finish."

Annie's smile disappeared as Steve limped off. "You don't have to bark at him." She stood, hand on hip, lips pursed in annoyance.

"He'll live." Jake peeled off his suit coat and hooked it over his left shoulder with one hand. "Come back to the house. I have news, but I'm too damned dry to talk."

"I'll get you a cold beer." She went ahead into the house. "Maybe it'll cool you down."

Jake followed, admiring Annie's feminine curves and tanned legs. She walked with an impatient bounce. He had the impression of a feisty mare giving the cold shoulder to a randy stallion.

Annie studied Jake as he came through the kitchen door. He appeared businesslike and too damned handsome in his dark trousers and white shirt. The top button was undone and his tie hung loose around his neck. Handing him the cold can of brew, she asked, "What's up?"

"Made a deal." He took a big swig from the can.

"Oh?" Annie waited.

"You remember your idea to take in paying guests."

"Dudes? You'll open the ranch to greenhorns? Let them work?" She chuckled. "I remember you nearly snapped my head off for suggesting it."

Ruefully, he smiled, "Changed my mind." Folding his arms, he propped one hip against the linoleum-topped counter. "I went into Prescott today. Talked with the loan officer at Desert Savings and Loan. Told him about your idea to open the ranch to people who'll pay to be cowhands for a week."

"But the bank at Dripping Springs turned you down." Annie stared at Jake, hope beginning to bloom.

"Henry Claybourne ran some figures, and said it could work." Jake reached her in two strides. He clasped her shoulders. "You did it, Annie. You found a way to get Rainbow back on its feet.'' He pulled her body against his powerful length, kissed her, then let go.

Startled, she lifted her gaze to Jake, and all her vows to keep a distance between them fell away in the gleam of his rich green eyes. A hungry ache uncoiled in her stomach. Her throat squeezed shut. Tears threatened because she knew, with a sharp pang of certainty, that she loved Jake, but she had no idea what the future might hold for her. Or for him.

She swallowed to clear her throat. ''When will work begin on the renovations?''

''Two days. The contractor figures to have the buildings ready by the end of July.'' Jake paused. ''Annie, we'll start with six greenhorns. It'll mean extra work for you. Maybe I can afford a raise to go with the work.''

''Hey, no problem. Cooking's my middle name.'' She grabbed a sponge and wiped down an already clean counter.

''Pack a lunch for both of us tomorrow. We'll ride to Wild Rose Canyon.''

She found a place needing extra attention. ''Rounding up strays? Checking trails?''

''A picnic.'' Jake tossed his empty can into the trash. ''You can help choose a good spot for the dudes to camp.''

''Aren't they coming to do ranch work?''

''Sure. I'll work their tails off, but we can sweeten the pot with a nice, relaxing campout at the end of their stay. Do some hunting and fishing, too—deer and wild turkeys.''

Annie felt her spirits lighten despite her misgivings. A whole day alone with Jake was worth the heartache. ''I'll be ready.''

Annie waited beside Sage in the corral as the first pink light of dawn spread across the eastern sky.

''Ready?'' Jake pulled up beside her, guiding a restless Bandit.

The stallion snorted and danced sideways, its ears twitching. Annie eyed the powerful horse, forcing back the familiar jolt of panic. ''Sure. Bring on the guided tour.''

She buttoned her jacket against the desert chill, gathered the reins, and swung into her saddle.

They rode side by side in the pale dawn. Clusters of red-coated cattle grazed in the short grass and shrubs.

Annie felt as if she and Jake were traveling a hundred years back in time in this harsh, quiet land.

After an hour's ride, Jake called a halt in the shade of tall, wind-carved rocks. Following his example, Annie drank a few sips of water while they looked back across the sweep of Rainbow land.

As the sun rose higher, Jake took the lead on a trail winding up the high plateau. Annie shifted, trying to ease the muscles in her legs and lower back.

Jake twisted in his saddle and studied her. "You hurtin'?"

"I'll keep up with you. If I'm able to do it, the dudes can, too." Annie gave him a cocky grin. "Lead on, Daniel Boone."

Midmorning Annie pulled to a stop beside Jake and looked out across the small valley below. Under the dome of crystalline blue sky, striated layers of red and white sandstone rose in concave cliffs on three sides. A green mosaic of trees and plants hid part of the valley floor.

"Wild Rose Canyon, first home of the Stone family." Jake's voice held a deep note of affection and pride. "My father used to bring me here. I'd always hoped to bring my kids."

He moved Bandit ahead of Annie and Sage, glancing back over his shoulder. "Trail's tricky. Let your horse pick the way."

She nodded, her mind filled with pictures of a little boy and girl with russet hair and green eyes in plaid shirts and jeans.

Man and horse went down a rocky path along the face of a cliff. Annie followed, forcing her attention away from a hopeless dream and back to the present.

On the valley floor, Jake reined in facing her. He took off his hat, and a warm breeze ruffled his hair. She saw the cool gleam in his eyes as he watched her.

He said, "Old homestead's up this side canyon." Turning, he followed a thin trail along a fast-moving stream. Riding beside him in the dappled shade of cottonwood and a few pine trees, she listened to the flirt and twitter of birds and the rustle of wind in the treetops.

"What do you think, Annie?"

"The guests will love it."

"Know how to do camp cooking, use a Dutch oven?"

"I can write my friend at the Flying C. They pack in for a week."

"Ask Verna. Before her husband died, he ran a big spread. Verna helped the chuckwagon cook."

Ahead, the stream flowed from a wide, sunlit pool. A tangle of arching rosebushes clustered at one end. Flat, sandstone slabs led to a small cabin sheltered by trees.

Annie stopped, entranced by the colors and fragrance. "Oh, Jake, are those the roses Elspeth Stone planted?"

"Family legend says she carried bare-root roses packed in moss from her home back east." He leaned out of the saddle, plucked a dainty, shell-pink rose, and gave it to Annie.

Holding the blossom to her nose, she breathed in its sweet, slightly peppery scent. "Your ancestors left you a wonderful legacy, Rainbow Valley, the ranch, all these—Jake!"

His arm wrapped around her back and side, hauling her halfway out of the saddle. Bandit bumped her leg. Her hat tumbled to the ground. Jake's mouth settled against hers, and she fought a losing battle against her own desire.

Sage moved restively. Jake's strong hand brushed Annie's fingers, grasping the reins. He kissed her with a fierceness that generated sensual shock waves through her whole body. Then, as swiftly as he'd pulled her into his embrace, he settled her back into the saddle, steadying her with one hand until she shrugged him away.

"Annie, thanks to you I'll keep all this."

Gratitude. Her stomach gave a sickening lurch. She should've realized he'd kissed her out of thankfulness. That was all. This wasn't love or anything remotely like it, she told herself sternly.

"It was just an idea. You got the plans going to make it work." Her voice trembled on the last words.

Annie fiddled with the reins. She had to get away before she betrayed herself. ''Aren't those wild turkeys past that crooked pine?''

''Yeah. Good eatin'.'' Jake stepped down from his saddle and bent to adjust the cinch.

She eased Sage into a walk toward where the big birds scratched and hunted for food in the deep grass, her thoughts more on Jake than guiding Sage.

A second flock of turkeys erupted from the underbrush. One huge tom spread his wings and flew at her.

The startled mare sidestepped nervously, almost falling, Annie clutched the pommel and regained her balance just as Sage took off with a leap, racing past Jake and Bandit into unfamiliar territory.

Jake shouted, ''Annie!'' She hadn't the breath to answer as she desperately fought to stay in the saddle and slow her mount's headlong flight. They splashed through a stream behind the cabin, dodged broken fence posts, and rushed heedlessly between trees and scattered boulders. Branches snagged her hair. Sage's mane whipped across her face, tangling in her eyelashes. The sharp smell of the mare's sweat filled Annie's nostrils. Tears of pain and fear stung her eyes.

She tried to regain control, but the spooked horse had the bit in her teeth and went faster, following the faint trail up a long bench of hard-packed earth and rock. The mare lunged at the steeper pitch and ripped the reins from Annie's hands. She watched with horror as the straps flew out of reach. How could she stop Sage from hurting them both? She didn't want to jump and leave the horse to injure itself.

Choking back her panic, she leaned forward, caught the flying reins, but lost her left stirrup. Her heel gouged the buckskin's side. With a wild snort, Sage charged up the narrow path, topped the crest, and raced into a shallow dip.

Too late, Annie saw the cliff ahead where land had collapsed into the valley. Frantic, she pulled at the reins. The mare made a sharp ninety-degree turn at the cliff's edge. Annie lost her other stirrup, tumbling sideways over her mount's shoulder. Her outflung fingers scraped rocks.

Then she felt herself falling through empty space.

Chapter Ten

Jake leaped from Bandit and raced to the crumbling edge.

Ten feet below, Annie clutched a dried out bush with both hands while her booted feet scrambled for a foothold on the unstable slope. As he watched, the roots pulled loose, and Annie slid another six feet in a rattle of loose rocks before crumpling onto a narrow granite shelf.

"Annie!" he shouted, fear churning in his gut.

She stretched out one hand, fingers tracing the outer side of the ledge.

"Don't move. I'm coming down."

In spite of his warning, Annie rolled toward the inside slope and propped herself up on one arm, only inches from a five-hundred-foot drop.

"Stay still, dammit!" he roared. Swiftly, he lashed one end of the rope to Bandit's saddle horn, went back to the edge, and lowered his lariat to dangle above her.

"Jake," she called in a shaky voice, "be careful."

He waved one hand to show he'd heard her, then inched down the cliff face, using cracks and outcroppings in the sandstone and shale for hand and toeholds. Pebbles showered around him. Hot midday sun beat down, making his fingers slippery.

Sweat dripped into his eyes, blurring his vision as he made intolerably slow progress.

"Watch out! That rock looks—"

The support gave way under his left boot in a clatter of shattering stone. He fought to keep his place, fingers aching, his whole body strung taut. Was Annie okay? Had the loose rocks hit her?

"Jake, hold on." Her voice had the high, thin sound of panic.

He breathed a little easier.

Another few feet and he crouched beside her on the narrow ledge. He brushed a smudge of red dirt off her pale cheek, silently cursing the scrape across the side of her face. "Break anything?"

"No." Cautiously, she lifted each arm, wiggled her fingers, and moved her legs. "See? It all works." She tried to grin.

"You'll be bruised and sore tomorrow." He bit off the last word. Fear still coursed through his blood and he grabbed her for a quick, harsh hug. "Listen to me. Do exactly what I say or you'll end up on those rocks down there."

Her face grew paler. Her eyes widened with fright, and she trembled under his hand. "I will."

With an economy of motion, Jake built a loop at the end of his lariat and settled it under her arms. "Know how to get loose when you reach solid ground?"

"Take the rope off. The guys taught me."

"Yeah." He remembered he'd chewed out Steve and Tomás for wasting time teaching her to throw a loop. "I saw you."

He checked the rope again. "Face the cliff. Use your hands and feet to protect yourself. Bandit's a good roping horse. He'll keep the line tight and pull you up."

"Got it, boss," she said, her voice laced with tension. She turned toward the cliff, one hand on the rope.

He signaled the stallion, calling, "Back up, back up." The rope grew taut. Bandit's hooves clicked on the thin dirt and rock above, as Annie made her climb up the steep slope.

After endless seconds, she shouted, "Made it," and the lasso end tumbled down to him.

When Jake crawled over the edge, he signaled Bandit to let

the rope slacken, then slipped loose. Annie stood beside Sage, rubbing the mare's withers. Jake felt her gaze focused on him.

She licked her lips and said, "Jake?" in a trembling voice.

"Later." He didn't dare talk to her until he contained his own helpless anger and fear. Only inches had saved her from death. The mental picture of her broken, lifeless body tormented him.

"Annie." His fingers shook as he touched her cheek. "Don't ever scare me like that again."

Her face was chalky. Her eyes still held a haunted look as she slowly shook her head.

With a groan, he closed his arms around her. She was safe. Nothing else mattered but the delicate woman shivering in his arms. Her skin felt clammy from shock. He held her tight against the heat of his body.

"God, Annie, when I saw you fall . . . "

She buried her face in his chest and clung to him. "I was terrified," she whispered.

He rubbed a hand up and down her spine, murmuring soothing words. When had she become so important to him?

A hot, resiny wind swirled across them, plucking at their clothes. Rocks and pebbles rattled down the cliff near their feet. The harsh cry of a hunting eagle drifted up from the void.

Annie stirred, then lifted her face to look into his. "I didn't act fast enough to stop Sage. She might've been injured or killed."

"*You* might have been killed." He tightened his arms around her.

A heavier gust of wind pelted them with fine sand. He turned with her to shield her face. "We have to get down to shelter before it really blows."

He quickly examined Sage's legs and feet for scrapes and cuts or sprain.

"Is she all right?"

With a sharp nod, he met Annie's eyes. "She'll do. Ready to get back in the saddle?"

"I'll have to," she said with a nervous laugh.

Admiring her courage, he boosted her onto the buckskin's

saddle and mounted Bandit. He looked back frequently to mark her progress as they went down the trail.

By the time they neared the cabin, Jake had his fear under control, but his skin still crawled at the memory of Annie going over the cliff.

He led her to a waterfall spilling from an opening high in the granite and sandstone wall. Mist curled from the pool at the base of the fall, cooling them in the midday heat. "Water's pure enough to drink here where it flows out of the cliff. Don't trust it later down the canyon."

She nodded.

Jake noted the bruises on her forehead. "We'll have lunch here. Wait. I'll lift you down."

Annie stared at him, clutching the reins. "I can do it myself."

She slipped her right foot out of the stirrup, but Jake was off Bandit and at her side before she got any farther. "Dammit, Annie, don't be so stubborn. You took a hell of a fall. It won't kill you to let me help."

He grabbed her around the waist, lifting her off Sage in one smooth motion. Her hands came down on his shoulders. Her sweet, firm body rested against him, and he realized he didn't want to let her go.

Settling her back on her feet, he unlashed a blanket from behind Bandit's saddle, and led Annie to a patch of shade under a cottonwood.

She caught his hand. "Jake, you save me today."

His stomach tightened at the memory. "Annie," he rubbed her shoulder. "You scared the hell out of me."

"And me—" Her voice broke on a sob. "Now my boots are full of gravel."

He knelt before her and pulled off her boots and socks. Looking up, he saw shadows in her eyes. A wave of protectiveness filled him. He drew her into his arms. "Annie." Resting his cheek on her hair, he gritted his teeth to ignore the hot, insistent throb in his groin.

"Jake," she sighed, leaning closer. Her warm fingertips threaded through his hair and danced on the nape of his neck. He quivered. Another rush of heated blood left him aching.

Tightening his hold, he traced her spine through the soft cotton shirt, down to her waist, then cupped her bottom. Her breasts flattened against his chest, her nipples hardening. He felt a jolt of primitive male satisfaction. She wanted him.

Annie closed her eyes. Jake's strength surrounded her, held her safe. She loved the heat of his body against hers, the feel of his hands. A bright, delicious tension swelled in her breasts, streaking like shafts of lightning to her lower stomach.

Nearby, the rush of water tumbling from the cliff made a pulsing background to the hot, tight dampness gathering between her legs. She felt secure in his arms, but she also knew why she hadn't said, "I love you," to Jake. What if he said nothing? His rejection would devastate her.

He carried her down to the wool blanket, braced his arms on both sides of her shoulders, and leaned over her. Above them, bright green leaves hung motionless in the afternoon calm, creating a pool of shade. Sweet grass and fallen leaves under the blanket cushioned their bodies, but all faded as she drowned in Jake's raw masculinity.

"I want you." He lowered his mouth toward hers.

"Yes," she whispered, tangling her fingers in his thick hair.

His lips touched hers lightly, brushed, teased, until she tugged at his head demanding more. He chuckled, a warm sound of approval, and slid one hand under her head, positioning her mouth for a harder kiss. Melting under the heat of his lips, she felt his fingers unbutton her shirt and spread it open. He traced the edge of her lacy bra, whispered, "Sexy," and tongued each nipple through the open weave.

She trembled at the intensely delicate sensation, and her fingers tightened in his hair.

He touched her tight nipples again with his teeth and she came partway up off the blanket, whimpering, "Jake," her body alive with an erotic fire.

"Easy, angel." He unfastened her bra and stripped it away with her blouse. A fitful breeze danced across her body, cooling her damp, sensitized skin.

Once more he settled his mouth on her lips—while his lean, tanned fingers caressed her—taking the kiss deeper, darker, to a level of passion she'd never known. He would be the first man she made love with. And the only one.

Annie tugged at his shirt buttons, popping them loose in her drive to touch, feel, taste, be closer to Jake. He gave a low growl of satisfaction, tossed aside his shirt, and tugged off his boots.

He settled one denim clad knee between her legs, nestling it at the top of her tight, aching thighs. God, she needed that pressure, that promise of relief. His hands, his lips, his tongue were lifting her, driving her higher, while the bright bands of passion coiled tighter, tighter, She dug her fingers into his shoulders and moaned, "Jake, help me!"

"Let go, honey." He unzipped her jeans and pressed his palm against her panties in the moist, full place where his knee burned. She called his name wildly—sobbing at the intense pleasure—and shattered into a thousand shards of incandescent fire. He held her tightly, one muscular leg over hers, his steely strength holding her together, keeping her safe at her most vulnerable moment.

She took a deep, shuddering breath and looked into his smiling eyes, about to murmur to him until he silenced her with a kiss, and skimmed off her jeans and panties. Still kissing her, he shucked the rest of his clothes, and settled between her legs.

His hands cupped her breasts, teasing them, pressing just the right amount to send her on another upward spiral. His lips joined his talented fingers, and soon Annie writhed under him, yearning for more, silently demanding all of him.

He twisted away to reach for his jeans, and for the first time Annie saw his full arousal. She caught her breath. She knew the mechanics, but how would they fit?

Jake turned back with a foil packet. He frowned. "Having second thoughts? God, I hope not." He kissed the side of her neck, whispering, "Last chance to say stop."

She caught his head between her hands, and guided his lips to her breast. "Don't stop."

"Annie, Annelise," he groaned, pausing before he resumed his erotic strokes, his sensuous touches.

Cool shade and hot drops of sunlight slipped across Annie's

bare skin. Jake's strong, powerful body loomed over her. She felt secure. His heartbeat throbbed like the distant waterfall, and his full, heavy arousal promised release for her desperate hunger.

She grasped the taut muscles on his back, silently urging him to join with her. His finger slipped into her sensitized flesh, and she gasped at the new sensation.

He muttered, "Damn, you're hot and tight," and slipped a second finger in. She moved her hips restlessly against his hand, craving more of the unknown electric flame crackling just out of reach.

White he stroked the very heart of her womanhood, Jake fastened his mouth on one breast and tugged at her nipple. She dug her nails into his flesh, lost in the blinding pleasure. He raised up, braced on hands and forearms, kissed her mouth hungrily, then surged forward, joining them in one stroke. She hadn't been prepared for the sudden sharp piercing invasion, and shuddered.

He froze. "What the hell? Annie?"

She held her breath, waiting for her body to adjust. "Go on. Finish it, Jake," she said on a high, breathless note.

He looked at her, eyes so dark with passion only a thin rim of green showed around his black pupils. "God, I can't stop," he groaned, and thrust again, building a newer, hotter spiral. His breath washed over her. His male scent, and the pulsing, hot sweetness of him inside her triggered a rippling spasm.

"Jake!" she gasped, and moved her hips to meet his intimate possession. Above her, his eyes were closed, his jaw tight. The muscles around his mouth and down his throat stood out in rigid cords. His shoulders flexed with coiled power. The pleasure he built in her grew higher until she cried his name and splintered apart in glorious release.

He surged deeper into her and went rigid, saying, "Annelise," in a heavy, choked voice. She caught her breath, so wrapped in his seductive spell she lost track of time as pleasure rolled through her in endless waves.

Trembling, he slumped against her. She held him while the

burning, sweaty enchantment he'd built in her rippled on and on.

Annie closed her eyes, cherishing their closeness. Still joined, she didn't want it to end. If only she could stay this way forever.

He moved as if to roll away.

"Jake, no. Wait."

He wrapped his arms around her and rolled over so she lay on top. Resting her cheek on his damp chest, she murmured, "I like this."

"Lady, lady." He played with one of her curls, winding it on his finger. "Ready to tell me why you were still a virgin? Hell, I'm not complaining, but you should've told me. I might've hurt you."

Annie stroked his chest, admiring the soft pelt of hair and the hard wall of his chest. "I never found the right man until I met you." She lifted her head, settled her chin on his breastbone, and grinned. "That was better than Death By Chocolate cake."

Jake touched the bruise on her cheek. His chest swelled with a new, overwhelming tenderness for her.

She'd been a virgin. The thought was like a punch in his gut. Why had he let his bitterness about his first wife's unfaithfulness blind him to Annie's innocence?

Annie's warm fingers traced the curve of his chin, and he leaned down and kissed her once more.

He cradled her head, strands of silky curls catching in his callused fingertips. Her sleek body molded to his. Her soft breath washed across his damp skin.

She murmured his name, and he felt even worse. She'd trusted him, but he'd betrayed that trust when he took her virginity. He'd even slipped the condoms into his pocket hoping to get lucky.

God, he should've realized why she was so tight, why she'd reacted as if it was the first time she'd experienced lovemaking. Because it was.

Jake felt lower than a snake, but the woman in his arms didn't have to know it.

Chapter Eleven

Annie whipped cheese into mashed potatoes, brooding about the letter Buck had handed her two hours earlier. It was the answer to a long-held dream, or was it?

The question troubled her all through the meal. She looked around at the crew, the men who'd become like brothers to her. Under the cover of serving food or eating, she studied Jake. Her feelings for him were far from sisterly.

After dinner, he helped with the dishes. "You're real quiet tonight. Hurting from the fall or from somethin' else?"

She blushed and couldn't meet his eyes, aware of sensual memories simmering between them—the press of skin against skin, the shattering pleasure of being in his arms. Her mind grew thick with yearnings. Her breasts swelled and crests tightened. She crossed her arms. "I'll take a hot bath and go to bed early."

For a moment longer, his look caressed her, then it vanished in a flicker of regret. His expression grew remote, unreadable as he dried a plate and put it on the stack. "Sleep in tomorrow. I'll fix breakfast. The men'll survive."

"There's something else on my mind." She submerged a handful of tableware, watching the soapy water bubble. "I wanted to discuss a job offer I got in the mail today."

His movements stilled. Slowly he picked up another plate and dried it. "A good one?"

"Incredible. Assistant to a world-class chef at Plumeria Bay Resort in Hawaii. Regency Enterprises runs it." Nervous, she rattled on, "The chef was a visiting teacher at the Cooking Institute. He asked for me."

"When do they want you?"

"That's the problem. The assistant had a mild heart attack. The letter said he's recovering, but his doctor told him to retire. Regency Enterprises wants me there in two weeks. I wanted to discuss it with you first."

Jake set the towel aside. "Pretty short notice."

"I know. With the contractors coming and later, the guests, I didn't want to leave you without a cook."

She watched for any expression of regret. Had the heat in Wild Rose Canyon been only that? Pure desire? Besides that question, her conscience prodded her. She'd signed a contract with Jake, and she'd never broken a promise. It was important for him to understand her motives.

She dried her hands and gestured toward the table. "Please sit. I want to tell you why the Regency job means so much to me."

"I'll stand."

Annie sank into a chair, torn by conflicting emotions. The chance of a lifetime. The head chef wanted her, but she loved the ranch and didn't want to leave it or Jake.

"All the years I worked to support Gabbie, all my studying at the Institute and working nights I've done to reach one goal. *Security.*"

"Go on." He propped one hip against the counter and reached for the mug of coffee he'd set aside before drying the dishes.

"You've lived on the ranch all your life. Do you know what it's like to come home from school and find the electricity turned off? Or going to bed early to save candles until Mom's next check, when the bill could be paid?"

He met her eyes. "No."

"When we got behind on the water bill, my sister and I'd

take turns watching for the man coming to turn off the water. We'd hurry to fill bottle after bottle before he arrived.''

Jake didn't say anything

To her dismay, she felt her eyes blur with tears. ''We had our pride, dammit. The one time Mom went to a state agency for help, they were so overworked, had so many people to see, she couldn't wait. She would've lost her part-time job.''

Annie blinked back the tears. ''Gabbie and I collected cans, bottles, anything we could sell. When I was twelve, I began baby-sitting to earn money.''

She glanced at Jake. He watched her with a dark expression on his face. ''Hey, we made it okay. Did you know supermarkets throw away perfectly good food? Gabbie and I would go dumpster diving. We'd lug home bread, rolls, cake, and lunch meat. I'd collect the limp veggies and fruits, pare away spoiled parts, and cook up vegetable soup or stewed fruit.''

Jake clenched the handle of his mug until Annie feared it would snap.

''The worst thing was sneaking away in the night with Mom and Gabbie, because the rent was overdue and we couldn't pay.''

He moved toward her. ''Annie. Don't.''

She put up a hand to stop him. ''No. I lied.'' Helplessly, she let the tears fall. ''The worst was the day I saw Mama die because she'd waited too long to go to the free clinic.''

Feeling Jake's arms slip around her as he knelt beside her chair, she leaned against him, absorbing his comfort.

''Take the job,'' he murmured, brushing his chin across her hair. ''I'll void the contract. Tell me when you want to leave. Your check'll be ready. I'll drive you to the airport.''

''Jake, I—''

He gave her a gentle kiss. ''Just do it.''

He stood, pivoted on his heel, and left.

Annie pushed to her feet and wearily climbed the stairs. How could she leave Jake just when he finally had a way to save Rainbow? The sweet passion they had shared would disappear quickly enough if they had to scramble every day to keep this ranch going. The Regency job was the opportunity of a lifetime.

She would never have to depend on anyone ever again. For anything.

Bathed and in bed, she tossed restlessly. Her dilemma went round and round, like a defective CD, repeating the same snatch of melody. The clock showed two-twenty before she drifted into an uneasy sleep.

By the time the contractor's crew and two truckloads of supplies arrived the next morning, Annie had finished her baking.

She went out to meet them and joined Jake on the porch. "Isn't it great? They're all set to start. Want me to make coffee? I have cookies ready."

He frowned. "They brought their own food. They're here to work."

"Of course, but it's a long drive from Prescott."

Jake gave her a searching look. "Go ahead, but don't give them any ideas."

"Are we back to that?" She felt something twist inside. In nine days she'd be gone, but she wanted Jake to trust her for the remaining time.

He stepped closer, one hand on the porch rail. She breathed in his heat and male scent. God, she wanted him.

"A couple of the guys in the crew think they're lady-killers. A woman smiles and they take it as a come-on. Plenty of ladies go for their type."

She moved back a step and hardened her voice. "Want me to make coffee?"

He studied her a moment longer. "Make coffee, but my advice is don't let them interfere with your work."

"I'll give you some advice, too, Jake. Go soak your head."

He clamped his battered Stetson on his head and strode down to where the contractor had collected his men.

The coffee was perked when Travis walked into the kitchen. "The boss sent me to help."

"To protect the workers from me?" Her lips thinned as she set out two platters of cookies and brownies.

"No, ma'am." Travis grabbed two brownies and devoured half in one bite. "He said to ride shotgun 'til they understood you're off limits. Rough characters."

"I don't know if I should be grateful or insulted."

Travis set his Resistol on one end of the counter and gave her a crooked smile. "You decide. The boss is pretty edgy today. Everyone's stepping light around him."

"What's that got to do with me?" Annie placed cups, cream, and sugar on a second tray.

"He said you were leavin' in a few days, and he sure wasn't laughin'."

"He knows my reasons."

Travis popped the last of the brownie into his mouth. Annie saw sympathy in his eyes.

"You love him, don't you, Annie?"

"Yes, but he'll never love me. He was too hurt by Stephanie to take another chance on getting close to a woman." Annie sighed. "He must've really loved her."

"Maybe at first, but that ended long before she died." Travis moved closer. "Jake 'n' me have been buddies since kindergarten. There's something you should know. Hell, everyone else in these parts does. Jake's mama hated Rainbow Valley. She left Stone and the kid three times."

"Three times? Why didn't she take Jake with her?"

"She wasn't a motherly kind of woman."

Travis took a molasses cookie and studied it. "Two times, Josh Stone left Jake with Verna to go get his wife and bring her home."

"Poor Jake must've been confused."

"That ain't the half of it. His mama was a beautiful gal who threw a party at the drop of a hat. And she sure liked the men. She pretty much ignored Jake unless she had an audience."

Annie imagined a bewildered little boy with said eyes. "No wonder Jake has a hard time trusting women."

"There's more." Travis polished off his cookie. "Jake just turned nine when she run off for the last time. Went with a rich man who wanted *her*, but not another man's brat. After she sent the divorce papers to Josh, he just stopped caring about her, or the ranch, or his son.''

A deep sadness for Jake welled up in her breast. Throughout her own childhood, her mother's love had been her rock. "It helps explain Jake's attitude."

"He's had some pretty raw experiences." Travis squeezed her shoulder. "Give him time. He'll come around."

"I only have nine days, Travis."

"I know." Travis picked up the heavy tray loaded with cups, sugar, cream, and the coffeepot and headed for the door.

Annie followed, her mind in a whirl.

As she went about her work, she pondered Travis's story. Jake had been betrayed by his mother and then by Stephanie. Still, at a critical time in his plans to save his beloved ranch, he was willing to give up Annie's help so she could have her dream.

How could she let him make that sacrifice? She suspected that she already loved him, but she knew she wasn't strong enough to sacrifice her own dream. And she wasn't ready to risk loving a man whose dream was a failing ranch.

Annie unpinned Jake's cotton shirt from the line and folded it on top of the wicker basket full of laundry.

For the last three days, she'd struggled with her decision to leave Rainbow—and Jake.

She plunked the basket on the porch and looked out across Rainbow Valley.

Sun Dancer whinnied and kicked up her heels as she raced around the pasture. Her patient mother ignored her antics.

Jake rode up the trail and turned toward the barn. Annie stopped herself from running to him. Even from this distance, he looked tired, but he'd avoided her since the night he told her to take the Regency job. Sometimes she caught him studying her intently. Was he hoarding memories the way she was doing?

Annie thought of the suitcases ready for her to pack. No. She couldn't do it. She couldn't leave Jake. Not now. She'd stay a little longer and help him out. She owed him that.

Chapter Twelve

Jake turned Bandit into the first corral and headed for the house, satisfied with the first two weeks of working guests on the ranch. Freshly painted buildings, the gleam of new fencing, and his expanded herd of horses grazing in the lower pasture, all pointed to success. He owed it to Annie. She'd talked him into trying the idea, had spent long hours decorating the guest quarters, and made everyone feel welcome.

A gust of wind snatched at his hat. He clamped it on his head and studied the heavy, oyster gray clouds building over the mountains.

Travis joined him. "Monsoon rains coming. Good for the range."

"Yeah. Better warn the greenhorns."

A burst of laughter from the patio in front of the guest houses caught Jake's attention. A group of dudes, most in new Western gear, watched Annie swing a lasso. Steve stood to one side, thumbs in his pockets, lazily talking to the young man assigned to him.

Travis nudged him. "Like old times, huh, Jake? Remember when this place had twenty guests for the weekend sometimes?"

Jake took off his hat, brushing back his hair as he surveyed the people lounging on chairs and benches or standing near the roping set-up. "That's was Ma's idea. She hated being alone on the ranch. Dad went along with her to keep peace."

"Didn't mean to rake up old hurts."

"No big deal. I don't miss her. She taught me some tough lessons. Too bad I forgot every one of them when I met Stephanie."

Annie's lariat circled the pole set up for practice, and she let out a delighted squeal.

"She's getting good." Travis shook out a cigarillo and lit it. "When she first started, she couldn't coil a rope."

Watching Annie show a male guest how to hold the lariat in his hands, Jake muttered a low-voiced curse and said, "She's too close." She bent to one side of the duded-up lawyer, her breasts nearly brushing the man's arm, her hips separated from him by a paper-thin distance.

Jake almost exploded. He sucked in a breath and clenched his jaw. "She's damn near in his pocket."

"Whoa, boss," Travis said. "Annie's entertaining your dudes because she's friendly and it's her job."

"Dammit, I know that, but do the dudes?"

Later, Jake, freshly showered and dressed, shuffled through the mail on his desk. He fingered a letter addressed to Annie. He looked at the company logo in the upper lefthand corner. Regency Enterprises.

He heard Annie's quick steps outside the office. She breezed in with with a friendly expression. "Jake, have you seen your grandmother's comb?"

"*Your* comb." Relieved to see her smile, he held it out by the bone teeth. The carved hummingbird on top reminded him of Annie, dainty but always on the go. Desire slammed into him. In spite of knowing better, he wanted her—now. "Found it beside the fireplace."

"Thanks." Her fingers brushed his hand. Heat rocketed through his blood. Refusing to lose control, he crossed his arms and leaned back in his chair.

She tucked a fall of ringlets away from her face with the antique comb. "I'll have to stop wearing it when I clean."

"Grandma wore it all the time."

"You're the boss." Reaching up, she touched the humming-bird.

He cleared his throat. "Annie, thanks to you, the guests are happy. I'd've put my foot in it a dozen times over. But you make them feel at home."

She laid her hand on his shoulder. Her leg brushed his and her sweet scent surrounded him. His entire body went taut with the effort not to interrupt the fragile peace growing between them. "New batch of guests settled?"

"Mrs. Potter-Sterns wants room service for dinner. Says she can't sit after her riding lesson today."

Jake studied Annie's impish smile. "No room service. You do too damn much now with eight guests and the crew.

"Travis can walk her to dinner. She acts like a cat in heat when any cowboy's around. You should see her when you walk by. It's amazing she doesn't burst into flames, or melt."

His iron control broke. He seized Annie's wrist and tumbled her into his lap. "Do you melt when I walk by, hmm?" He nuzzled her neck.

"Like butter in a hot skillet." She curled against him, one hand slipping around his side, her head thrown back. "You're one tasty hunk, Jake."

He supported her pliant form with his left arm. "Want a sample?" He nibbled at her lips and took her mouth in a hot, intimate kiss. Her tongue tangled with his. She tasted of cinnamon and honey and . . . Annie.

Desire raced through him as he cupped her breast, feeling the heat of her skin through the cotton knit. He slid his thumb across her sensitive peak, and she arched toward him, her fingers digging into his side.

"God, Annie, I want more."

"Jake," she said in a choked voice. "Not here. Someone could walk in."

"Yes, here. Door's closed," he breathed, and gripped the hem of her T-shirt.

Outside, voices raised in argument grabbed his attention.

"You gol-darn sidewinder. I told you not to open the gate between Bandit's corral and Estrella." Buck sounded truly furious.

"Who the hell are you to give me orders? I'm a guest. I'll do what I damned well please."

Jake had one glimpse of Annie's flushed face as she scrambled to her feet.

"Stay here, out of the way." Jake strode to the door. "Estrella's coming in season, but she's not ready for Bandit. She might kick the hell out of him."

Jake drove the troublemaker into Prescott and returned after dark. He nodded to the guests gathered on the porch with their after-dinner coffee. As he headed toward the kitchen, the tantalizing odor of roast beef grew stronger.

He paused to watch Annie wash a stack of salad plates. Her work had doubled since the guests had arrived, even with Sally Sloan to clean the extra rooms, but she never complained.

"I'll order a dishwasher tomorrow. Want help tonight?"

She turned, smiling at him. "A dishwasher will be terrific. Go ahead to the dining room. I kept your dinner warm. I'll bring the salad."

He sat at the kitchen table. "Here's fine. I like the view."

"You mean you like to watch someone work." She pulled a salad from the refrigerator and set it in front of him.

While he ate, he discussed the day with Annie. Stephanie had yawned and studied her perfect nails at the details of running the ranch, but Annie listened and asked all the right questions. Jake treasured these quiet evening discussions, suddenly aware they'd become a bright spot in his life. God, he'd miss them when Annie left.

After dessert, he brought the letter to her where she sat at the small table, finishing a cup of coffee. He sat across from her and waited.

Looking puzzled, she opened the letter murmuring, "What do they want now?" Slowly, she read the letter, then stuffed it back in its envelope. Her voice went very thin and flat. "Regency has another position for me when my contract here is finished."

She glanced at the calendar hanging beside the mudroom door. Her eyes sought his. Time was running out. The unspoken thought hung in the air. Jake felt a savage acceptance, almost a cruel relief as his fear came true. She'd probably known about this for a while and hadn't wanted to tell him. She'd leave. First his mother, then Stephanie. Soon it'd be Annie.

As if to punctuate his thoughts, the gathering storm speared Rainbow Valley with lightning. Thunder rolled across the night, rattling windows. A rising wind caught the heavy rain, flinging it against the glass panes.

He muttered a curse, not sure if it was directed at the storm or his dark thoughts.

"Jake—"

He jerked away from her outstretched hand and left the kitchen as if pursued by Old Sin.

Warmhearted, generous, giving, Annie was everything he'd always wanted in a woman. He was falling in love with her. But, dammit, he'd never again love a woman who'd walk away from Rainbow, walk away from him.

Annie drove into Dripping Springs to pick up her grocery order, stopping first at the Coffee Cup Cafe. Waving to Gus as she walked in, her cook's nose told her he'd finally changed the grease in the fryer. The same two old cowhands who seemed to spend their days at the counter politely touched the brim of their hats. She smiled a greeting.

"Annie, just in time for my break." Verna poured two cups of coffee, put one in front of Annie, and slid into the booth across the table from her. "I'm glad you came in. I've got something to tell you."

"You won the lottery?"

Verna grinned. "Better 'n that." She held out her left hand. "Buck popped the question."

"You're engaged. That's great!" She grasped Verna's fingers to get a better look at the diamond set in an open gold heart. "I'm thrilled for you and Buck."

"Yep. 'Bout time the old coot asked. I swear, he was the behindest man I ever saw when it came to declarin' his intentions."

She stared at her ring a moment, moving her fingers so the gem flashed, then reached out and squeezed Annie's hand. "Honey, I've come to care a whole lot for you. I think of you as the daughter I never had. Will you stand up with me, be my maid of honor at the wedding?"

Tenderness tinged with sorrow flowed over Annie. Her happiness for Verna tangled with her sadness over Jake. She rested her hand on Verna's. "I'd be honored."

"Good. Wedding's next Sunday, right after the service."

"So soon? I better shop for a dress tomorrow."

"Got mine already." Verna grinned. "Buck and I waited too long to get married for us to delay the ceremony."

She got a fresh pot of coffee, refilled their mugs, and sat across the table from Annie again. "How're things at Rainbow? Jake behavin' himself?"

"He's okay." Annie wrapped her fingers around the cup, and developed a sudden interest in the curve of the handle—anything to distract herself from her wistful feelings.

Verna set her cup down. "That fancy Mrs. Potter-Sterns came in last week with Steve. She was rubbin' against him like a cat with an itch, if you know what I mean, but he moved away and told her about Monica. Didn't seem to put her off any." Verna covered Annie's fingers with her work-worn hand. "She chasin' Jake, too?"

"She tries. He's polite to her, but he keeps his distance."

"Ain't no surprise." Verna tucked a loose strand of black hair under her fine hairnet. "The way Stephanie flirted with everything in trousers made Jake pretty immune."

"Stephanie again." Annie sighed and stared into her cup of strong, black liquid. "Why do memories of her hang around like a bad smell? The kind all the vinegar, lemon juice, and air freshener in the world won't get rid of."

Verna sipped her coffee. "She was real pretty. Men just

naturally took to Stephanie. Ben and Jake both courted her, but I guess you know that.''

''I heard that she and Ben met in secret even after she married Jake. Why on earth did she ever marry him, anyway?''

''Ben weren't so rich then. Old man Stone's Rainbow Valley Ranch looked more prosperous. Of course Stephanie didn't know Jake's dad was pilin' up debts.''

''If I had to choose between Jake and Ben, I'd pick Jake any day.''

''No contest. Jake's always been worth ten of Ben Russell.''

Fidgeting in the seat, Annie looked straight into Verna's eyes. ''I hate to pry into Jake's past, but his hot and cold attitude hurts. What was the mystery surrounding Stephanie's death?''

''There was no mystery, honey. It just hurt Jake terribly to know his wife was fooling around with another man.'' Verna's eyes filled with compassion. She rested one hand on Annie's arm. ''Three years ago, Stephanie was running away to Ben Russell. She got trapped when Gold Creek flooded the road. By the time Jake found her, she'd drowned.''

Chapter Thirteen

"Buck's late for breakfast. Is he sick?" Annie set a bowl of scrambled eggs on the table and poured coffee for everyone.

"Yeah, lovesick." Steve added a slab of ham to his plateful of pancakes. "He staggered in late with lipstick smears and a silly smile on his face."

Jake put the syrup pitcher down. "He sure as hell better get in here and eat, or he'll spend the morning working hungry."

The kitchen door opened. Buck strutted in, his wet boots leaving tracks on the polished floor. "Don't get your feathers in a ruffle, Jake. I ain't usually late. Besides, I've got somethin' to announce."

"Spit it out."

"Since you asked so polite-like." The old wrangler's grin included everyone at the table. He winked at Annie. "Verna and me are getting married."

There was a stunned silence, then the crew exploded in laughter.

"Married? An old coot like you?" Steve said with a guffaw. "Hell, you had me goin' for a minute."

"It's no joke, Steve. If you wuzn't wet behind the ears, you'd believe me."

Jake eyed Buck skeptically. "She finally caught you, huh?"

"I asked her." Eyes crinkling with mirth, the groom-to-be piled food on his plate and reached for the butter.

With a wry smile, Travis said, "Well, I'll be damned. Another one bites the dust."

Ignoring him, Buck waved his fork. "You're all invited. We'll have eats afterward in the Fellowship Hall. Verna said Annie will make the cake."

"I'm coming." Steve reached for the insulated carafe and topped off his mug. "Ain't every day we can eat Annie's cake at a hitch-n-brand wingding."

Travis motioned to Steve for a refill. "Hell, the church roof'll collapse when I walk in, but I'll be there."

Annie went to Buck and kissed his cheek. "Congratulations. Verna told me yesterday. I'm happy for both of you."

Buck clasped one of her hands. "Verna's real fond of you. Me, too. If'n I'd had a daughter, I'd a wanted her to be sweet and good like you."

"You and Verna are special to me," Annie said, touching Buck's weathered jaw. "Now start eating before those bandits steal your food. I have something in the kitchen."

The good-natured ribbing continued as she refilled everyone's glass with freshly squeezed orange juice, and raised hers in a toast. "Here's to a joyous wedding, and a long and loving marriage."

The old cowboy swallowed a mouthful of liquid, studying Annie and Jake with a sly grin. "I ain't naming names, but there are a couple of others here who should be thinking of tyin' the knot."

Annie felt her cheeks grow warm. Buck patted her shoulder. "What do you think, Jake?"

Jake's chair scraped. Startled, Annie's gaze flew to him in time to see him fix her with a frigid stare. "Nothin' doin', Buck. If I get married again, it'll be a business deal with no illusions."

Sunday came with a rush. Buck and Verna's wedding day had arrived.

Annie steeled her heart for facing Jake across the nave of the church. Buck had talked him into being his best man, but Jake hadn't looked any too happy about it. She hoped he'd at least put a good face on things for the wedding.

Driving toward the Gold Creek bridge in bright sunshine, Annie mentally counted her remaining time at Rainbow Valley. Three weeks until she left to take the position Regency Enterprises had offered her. Just thinking of the short time before she said goodbye forever left a hollow place inside her.

At the church, Annie sighed. Couples everywhere.

As if conjured up by her thoughts, Jake stepped out of Travis's truck, and Annie's mouth went dry. He wore a black suit, a fine cotton shirt, and a subtle gray and black tie. Sunshine glinted on the amber and gold in his russet hair.

She smoothed her pale blue dress, conscious of the intensity of his gaze. He came toward her with the measured pace of a predator. Mentally she shook herself. This was Jake, not someone she should fear, but her skin still tingled at his approach.

"Annie." He nodded. "You look nice."

"So do you." Trying to hide the tremor in her fingers, she slid them under his lapel to pin on a pink rosebud. At the brush of her hand on his jacket, he went rigid. Standing so close to him, she felt his heat and smelled the clean scent of soap and male. It brought back memories of his naked body pressed against hers on the blanket in Wild Rose Canyon, and her hand shook even more. Finally she fastened the boutonniere.

"Finished?" His voice sounded low and strained.

She stepped back. "You're the last one."

He wrapped his hand around her elbow. "I'll escort you into church."

Caught in the pleasure of his touch, she walked beside him to the front pew where Verna sat with the pastor's family.

Jake settled beside Buck in the pew across the aisle from Annie. He kept his gaze away from her, but her appearance was already fixed in his mind. As she'd stood in front of the church, a warm desert wind had pressed her light, silky dress against her slender form, molding it to her hips and breasts. The curved neckline, trimmed with lace, had framed her slim neck and face. Jake took a deep breath. His own memories of Wild Rose Canyon tantalized him. He clenched his teeth, forcing his attention to the present.

After the short sermon, it was time for the wedding. Jake took his place beside Buck and watched Annie walk down the aisle carrying a small bouquet of pink and white flowers trimmed with blue ribbon. Her red gold hair was partly held by the hummingbird comb. Jake was touched. She looked as pretty as a bride. He squelched the thought.

Buck murmured, "Verna." Jake looked at the back where Gus, dressed for once in a suit, escorted the bride.

As Buck took Verna's arm and they stood before the altar, Jake face Annie. He heard the pastor say, "Friends, we are assembled here in the presence of God to unite Buckminster Carleton Mathews and Verna Edith Wilson in marriage."

Jake's thoughts went back to the lavish ceremony and expensive banquet Stephanie had demanded. That should've been a clue to her expectations. At the time, he'd been too blinded by lust and his own ego. After all, he'd beat out Ben Russell for her hand.

The pastor continued, but Jake focused on Annie standing so sweetly solemn to one side. Somehow he knew she'd prefer the simplicity of a country wedding like Buck and Verna's.

"Will you promise to love, honor, trust, and serve her in sickness and in health, as long as you both shall live?" the pastor recited.

Jake heard his old cowhand friend say, "I do." Looking at Annie, he thought, *I do love her, but—hell, it'll never work. She wants a career, and she'll be leaving in a couple of weeks.* He'd be damned if he'd be abandoned again. Jake curled one hand into a fist. *God, it hurts.*

Annie took a breath. Her emotions were in turmoil—happiness for Verna and Buck, quiet yearning for a man she couldn't have. They'd reached the time to exchange rings. Annie took Verna's bouquet, and her gaze settled on Jake. Her heart gave a jolt. For a brief moment, he'd looked at her with a wistful expression. Now he seemed remote again. She sighed. He just wasn't the marrying kind.

Somewhere in the congregation, a baby cooed and burbled. Annie saw indulgent smiles on the adults' faces. The proud father shifted the infant to his broad shoulder. She realized how much these people had welcomed her into their community, had given her acceptance and friendship. She belonged here, wanted to stay, to put down roots. Have babies of her own.

With a start, she realized that Buck had placed the wedding ring on Verna's finger. Now it was Verna's turn. Annie placed the heavy band of gold in her friend's hand.

Verna slid the ring on her groom's finger, saying, ''Buck, with this ring I pledge my live and love to you.''

Annie felt her attention helplessly drawn to Jake. For a single, shining moment, she pictured herself making her own pledge to him. Lord, it would be heaven. Her love for him grew deeper every day, but her stay at Rainbow Valley would end too soon. Her throat clogged with emotion. How could she leave when her heart was here?

The wedding potluck went on long into the afternoon. Some of the livelier guests gathered around a fiddle player and started an impromptu square dance on the lawn in front of the little church.

Annie followed the calls as best she could, laughing with her partners until Jake cut in for good, refusing to swing her away to any other man.

He let her go finally, happy and exhausted, to flop on the grass beside Verna, as he went off in search of more champagne.

''Annie, that man's crazy about you. He's not the kind to come right out and say so, but anyone can see it. You know I waited a long time for Buck . . . he teased and joked around a lot, and I didn't know if he'd ever be serious. Now we're going to have our happiness before it's too late. You should do the same.''

''I'm so happy for you.'' Annie hugged her. ''Buck's an old dear, and you've been my friend from the first moment I walked into the cafe. Jake's a different story. I'm crazy about him. If he loved me and asked me to stay, I'd say yes so fast he wouldn't know what hit him."

Annie pushed a strand away from her face and tucked it behind her ear, struggling to hide her breaking heart. "Now that it's too late, I realize the only security I need is Jake's love."

"Jake's a good man, but he's awful wary." Verna patted Annie's hand. "I hope he hasn't been too tough on you. He gets that way sometimes."

"We only have to put up with each other for two more weeks."

Jake saw Annie and Verna deep in conversation and tactfully kept his distance. Her hair was loose, tumbling over her shoulders, aglow in the light of late afternoon.

Buck appeared at his side with an empty glass, looking for a refill.

Jake upended the bottle he carried into Buck's glass. "One more, old friend? Seems your bride's had enough partying. She's over there with Annie."

"I'm ready to take her home. We've already wasted too many years." Buck took a final sip and set the glass on a nearby table. "Boss, what's with you and Annie? Any fool with half a brain can see you care about each other. Ask her to stay. Marry her."

"I got no luck with women." He laughed. "Slippery little devils. Can't hang onto 'em. So I won't try anymore."

"Jake, you're a stubborn fool." Buck stalked off toward Verna.

Buck's right. Jake thrust his hands into his pockets and watched Annie kiss Verna and Buck on the cheek. He felt more alive with Annie around than he ever had before.

He loved her, but how could he risk everything on a woman? If he lost out this time it would kill him.

Chapter Fourteen

Jake stared at the computer screen. After he'd kicked so hard against dudes staying at Rainbow, the figures on the monitor showed it was a real gold mine.

Thanks to Annie, the ranch was back on its feet. He wished he could say the same for himself.

A knock sounded on the door and Travis sauntered in. "Boss, everything's buttoned down for the night. All the dudes've hit the sack, and Annie went upstairs an hour ago."

"I'll see you at breakfast."

Instead of leaving, Travis crossed to the table where Annie had left a tray of refreshments and extra mugs. He poured himself a cup of coffee, grabbed a handful of peanut butter cookies, and sprawled in an armchair facing Jake. "Hear we have four new guests coming in tomorrow."

"A family. Nick'll get them."

Frowning, the blond ramrod munched on a cookie. "More work for Annie."

"It's her job. Something stuck in your craw?"

"Hell, yes." Travis leaned forward. "Jake, you've been actin' like a bear with a sore paw. You would've insulted half the guests, if it weren't for Annie steppin' in. When she does, you turn on her like a grizzly defendin' its territory.''

"I'm still the boss.'' Jake surged to his feet. "Even though she damn near runs the place. Everybody loves her. The food is so good the hands are getting spoiled.'' He paused, shoved one hand through his hair, and muttered thickly, "What the hell will I do when she leaves?''

"That's what I thought.'' Travis smiled in understanding. "You can't stomach the idea of Annie going.''

Jake dropped into the other armchair, cupping his face in his hands briefly. His eyes lit on the tray Annie had left and he felt a now familiar sense of loss. "But she is.'' He closed his eyes tight. "She's the reason Rainbow is prospering. But I hate being so damned beholden to her.''

"Is that really what's on your mind?''

"God, Travis, what do you want—blood? I like Annie. She's fun and smart. She's worked hard to fit in. She's learned to ride, and she's turned into a great trail cook.'' Silently he added, *and I need her so badly it hurts.*

"Tell her.'' Picking up the carafe, Travis refilled both mugs and returned to his chair.

Minutes passed. A horse whickered to its stablemates. In the distance, a coyote called in the night. Another one answered. Two more joined in. Gradually the calls faded away. Even coyotes have mates, Jake thought bleakly.

"Sounds like they're headed toward North Basin.''

Jake hid his startled reaction to Travis's voice. "I'll send Tomás out tomorrow to check on the small herd there. He can take Clint and David. They haven't worked that section yet.''

Travis stood and stretched.

Standing, Jake gripped his friend's shoulder. "I'll talk to Annie in the morning.''

Annie checked the last guest room off her list. Then she headed out, enjoying the gentle warmth of the early morning sunshine, to say hello to Sun Dancer.

Jake called to her from the barn, and she changed direction

to meet him, her sneakers crunching on the newly graveled path. After days of him keeping his distance, she was delighted by his friendly smile.

"Annie, you've been hard at it since early dawn."

"Just doing my job, boss," she drawled.

"You've done a helluva lot more." With a fleeting, wistful expression, he touched her cheek. "The dudes could've canceled because of the rains. You convinced them it was an adventure to slog through mud chasin' cattle. Take a break. Go to Prescott with me tonight for dinner."

"What about the guests and crew?" Annie silently cursed her own sense of responsibility. "Better give me a rain check."

"We'll leave right after they eat. Have a late meal." A slow smile played around his lips. "Wear something dressy."

"You're on." Annie ran back to her room, rapidly making plans. She'd set her hair. Hold back the curls with the hummingbird comb. With a start, she realized that it wasn't on her dresser. Had she lost it at the wedding?

That evening, Annie walked down the stairs, feeling very feminine for a change, in a softly fitted, jade green dress. With each step, the slinky material brushed and flared around her knees.

Jake appeared in the arched doorway from the living room. His tailored, navy-blue suit emphasized the masculinity of his powerful body and set off his deeply tanned skin. His eyes glowed with appreciation as he held her light jacket for her. "Purtiest biscuit-pusher in the whole dang west," he drawled, imitating Buck.

She pretended to simper, glancing at him sideways through lowered eyelashes. "Why, thank you kindly. I swear, you take my breath away."

Smiling, he opened the door for her, and she walked out into the cool desert night.

He gently assisted her into the new ranch pickup and started the engine.

High beams glared against trees lining the road. The eyes

of night creatures reflected the light like tiny green jewels. Slowly Annie relaxed, enjoying the ride through the quiet valley with Jake.

"Annie, you look good enough to eat." The genuine admiration in is voice sent a throb of pleasure through her.

"You clean up pretty good, too, Jake."

"Determined to give our evening the light touch, aren't you?"

"It's better this way. We both know I won't be here much longer."

"Friends?" He patted her hand.

Fighting the sensual awareness his touch generated, she shook it. "Friends."

For the remainder of the trip, they sat in companionable silence or reminisced about the months she'd been at Rainbow. By tacit agreement, they avoided mentioning Wild Rose Canyon.

From the moment they entered the new restaurant in Prescott, Annie enjoyed its subdued, elegant decor. They were shown to a table beside windows overlooking a moonlit garden. The indoor lights were low. Centered on a snowy tablecloth, a candle flickered in an amber globe. A combo played mellow, danceable music.

After the waitress took their order, Jake lifted his glass of wine to Annie in salute. "To the best gourmet cook who ever tamed a bunch of cowhands."

"That's not what you said the first time you saw my corn bread tamale pie." She grinned at the memory of that meal.

"I was trying to forget the sight of you chasing my cattle." Jake's warm fingers clasped her hand, his thumb brushing the inside of her wrist. "Annie, I gave you plenty of hell on the ranch, but you've helped me make a go of it. Those greenhorn guests have paid the bills and let me move ahead."

"Great news." With an effort, she hid the lurch of excitement his touch generated. "But you'd better give back my hand. The waitress is coming with our soup."

His lips twisted into a wry smile as he dropped her hand. "Dance with me later? As friends, of course."

"Of course." Annie spooned up a mouthful of curry soup, but she barely tasted it.

During the rest of the meal, Annie did her best to ignore the appeal of his compelling green eyes, the set of his rugged shoulders, even the admiring smile lurking around his lips. Mentally, she berated herself for letting her attention linger on his mouth. Memory quickly supplied the feel of those lips on hers. She wanted to moan. Her good intentions were rapidly proving the old saw of paving the road to hell. With Jake, she wanted more than friendship. She desired—

"Dance?"

Jolted out of her thoughts, Annie gazed at his outstretched hand. "I'd love that." She rose to meet him.

He followed her to the small dance floor, his warm fingers linked with hers. At the edge of the polished parquet, she went into his arms with the naturalness of a bird returning to its nest.

She closed her eyes and let the music and the rhythm of his heartbeat take her.

Jake had managed to keep his hands from straying as they'd danced, and now he lay awake berating himself. There wasn't much to be said for being a perfect gentleman.

After a shower, he lay in bed, clad only in a towel, trying to distract himself from the sweet temptation only a few strides down the hall.

He cocked his head, listening to a soft footfall outside his door. The door opened soundlessly, and he quickly made sure he was more or less decent.

A slim figure stood in the doorway, her hair a soft halo in the dim hall light.

"Jake?" She hesitated, clutching her old pink bathrobe closed against her throat, then stepped into the room. "You awake?"

"Something wrong?"

She advanced halfway across the room and waited. "I can't sleep."

"Not a good idea to come in here."

"I want to be with you." Tension threaded her voice. "Don't make me beg."

Silently he pulled the cover aside in invitation. When she didn't move, he held out one hand. "Annie."

She flew toward him and dropped to her knees on the mattress, close enough for him to smell her elusive fragrance. "I was afraid you'd send me away."

"I should." His body urged him to grab her, take what she offered. "I can't give you love or marriage."

A lightning burst illuminated her expression of uncertainty. She whispered, "I know."

In the deeper darkness following the bright glare, he heard her sobbing intake of breath. Damn, he thought bitterly, I've hurt her. Not that he hadn't done it before, but this time he knew he wasn't dealing with a flirt.

"Jake?" Her fine-boned hand spread on his shoulder, and slid up to his jaw.

Fighting the urge to pull her to him and ease his aching need in her yielding body, he covered her soft, cool fingers with his. "Last chance to change your mind."

"Afraid to get hot and sweaty?" Annie leaned over him, the top of her bathrobe open, displaying pale, gleaming skin.

He nudged the robe farther apart, remembering the feel, the scent of the shadowed valley between her breasts.

"Gonna make me eat my words?" Lifting his head, he licked the tempting flesh, savoring its slight saltiness and the musky sweetness of the rose lotion she used. "God, honey, you taste like heaven."

Sighing his name, Annie sprawled on top of him. He untied her belt, slipped his arms under the robe, and closed them around her. They lay skin to bare skin, heat against heat, desire against aching desire. Only her lacy panties made a thin barrier.

Annie's fingers trailed down his side to his flank, sensitizing his skin. Her hand clutched his buttocks, while she nuzzled against his chest. He groaned, trying to control the hot lust roaring through him. Sure as hell if he gave in to it he'd scare her.

Her lips brushed his throat and nibbled across his chest. He shivered, waiting for her to reach his male nipples. She chuckled, a low, satisfied sound. "Makin' you crazy, Jake?" she drawled.

"Where'd you"—she kissed one nipple and his whole body clenched—"learn that?"

"From you," she purred, trailing a finger back and forth across both sensitive points. "You're a good teacher. Am I a good student?"

"Yes," he growled, reaching for her hand. "My turn—"

"Wait." She silenced him with a finger across his lips, sat up, and straddled his hips. The sheer fabric of her panties rubbed in seductive friction against his flesh.

She cradled his face with her hands, nibbling, teasing his mouth. The kiss went on and on as fire coursed through his blood and throbbed in his rigid sex.

He stripped the robe from her shoulders, tossed it aside, and fondled her petal-soft breasts.

She circled his wrists with her fingers, tugging gently. "I'm in charge."

Amused by her boldness, he let her pin his writs to the bed on both sides of his head.

"Good boy," she aid with a sexy grin, then rocked forward. Slowly, she rubbed her breasts against his chest, igniting a greater storm in him. Again and again, she moved. Ecstasy, on the edge of pain, raced through his body while he slowly twisted and groaned under her sweet sensual assault.

Her female moisture dampened him. The scent of her readiness filled his nostrils.

"Enough!" He slipped his fragile bonds, tore the fabric separating them, and, clasping her hips, lifted and settled her on his arousal.

She wiggled, adjusting to his penetration. Her smooth sheath clasped him. Streams of pulsing heat pumped through his sex. Above him, Annie rode with her head flung back, eyes closed. Her movements quickened, and her skin glistened with passion.

He matched the thrust of his hips to her rhythm, building higher, hotter, deeper.

As her inner muscles tightened, he knew her peak was near.

His own was building to the flashpoint, until she sobbed his name and he felt her passionate release. Then he exploded, and groaned her name.

Annie lay draped along the length of his body. Jake held her with a new tenderness. He'd never dreamed a woman could be so giving, could make him feel the depths he'd known tonight.

In the intimate shelter of his bedroom, Jake kissed the top of Annie's head, wondering how he could watch her leave Rainbow.

She whispered, "I'll have to give you an *A* for awesome."

"You were wonderful." He feathered a kiss on her closed eyelids, and rubbed the base of her spine where it curved into her seductive bottom.

Easing out of her, he settled her at his side, one arm around her waist.

Murmuring, "Jake," Annie snuggled her head on his chest, fingers spread across his muscles. "I should move, but you're better than any pillow."

Reaching down, he found the summer quilt and pulled it up over both of them. "Go to sleep, honey," he muttered, stroking her hair.

The steady sound of raindrops lulled them both to sleep.

Chapter Fifteen

"Magic." Jake stroked the curry comb down Bandit's side, trying to hide his own silly grin. Last night Annie had worked magic every time she touched him. Hell, he grew hard just thinking about it.

Jake grabbed the assignment clipboard from its hook beside the door. All the guests were gone with their crew members.

He wanted Annie in his arms again. With her words, her laughter, her touch, she filled up the emptiness inside him, and made him a happy man once more.

Outside, Lady whinnied to her foal. Bandit snorted, and Jake rested one hand on the stallion's shoulder. "How do you court *your* favorite mare, old boy?" He watched dust motes dance in a shaft of sunlight, and remembered last night. He wanted— needed Annie's bright enthusiasm and passion. She had to stay here, with him, remain a part of this land he loved.

The sound of an engine alerted Jake to visitors just as a white and gold Range Rover came into sight past the trees screening the curve.

He left the barn, cutting across the lawn to the house. Uneasiness prickled the hair on the back of his neck. It changed to anger when the truck parked and Ben Russell stepped out.

Jake planted himself between Russell and the ranch house. "Get your ass back in the truck before I toss it there."

Ben took two steps toward Jake, his boots crunching in the gravel. "I came to see Annie."

"Hit the road, or it's you and me, Russell."

Ben took something out of his shirt pocket and twirled it in the sunlight. "Let Annie decide. She's a more welcoming sort of woman—kind of like Stephanie."

Before Jake could take a step, the screen door banged. Annie clattered down the stairs and stopped beside him.

"Russell?" Color drained from her face as she stared at the object Ben held.

"Lose something?" Ben asked with a knowing smile.

"How'd you get my hummingbird comb?" Annie reached for it, but Ben moved back, chuckling.

Jake stepped between Ben and Annie. "Gettin' light-fingered, Russell? Give back the comb and haul your sorry butt out of here."

Ben looked over Jake's shoulder, ignoring him. "Why, Annie, I'm a gentleman. I don't kiss and tell."

"There's nothing to tell, you, you—" Annie sounded too choked by indignation to continue.

Jake felt a terrible rush of bitterness at the meaning of Ben's words. "Dammit, Ben, a rattlesnake is more of a gentleman than you."

"Get out of my way, Stone. This is between Annie and me."

"Like hell it is. This is my land. She works for me." He felt Annie move up beside him and put an arm around her shoulder. "She gets my protection."

"Jake," she murmured.

Ben's eyes narrowed. "You're sleeping with her."

Jake felt Annie's subtle movements to pull away from him without Russell seeing the effort. He tightened his grip. "There's nothing here for you, Russell. Give her the comb and hightail it."

"That's why I came." Ben handed the comb to Annie. "See you later, sweetheart."

"I'm not your—"

"Move!" Jake lunged at Russell, spun him around, and shoved him toward the Range Rover.

Ben caught his balance against the door and climbed inside. He started the engine, then threw a kiss to Annie before driving off.

Annie grabbed up a handful of gravel and threw it at the Rover, yelling, "Don't come back."

Seething with anger, Jake took a deep rasping breath. His pulse hammered in his throat. He felt betrayed, so furious he couldn't speak. Turning away from the woman he'd come to love, he slammed his fist into his open hand. She whispered his name and he shuddered. When would he learn?

Annie had seen Jake's face harden at Russell's innuendoes. She'd been helpless to stop the destructive words. Her palms grew clammy. A wave of acid welled up in her stomach. She clutched the hummingbird comb, wishing the whole scene had been just a bad dream.

He still had his back to her. Did he condemn her because of Ben?

Suddenly Jake swung around. Coldly he looked at her. "Why couldn't you just stay away from the man? The day you came to work for me, you promised you wouldn't have anything to do with Russell. Next thing I knew, you were sneakin' around my back to his ranch."

"I went to see my friend Darryl. No law against that. Unless you think it's your business what I do once my work's done."

"Actually, I do. But you don't have to concern yourself with what I think."

She threw back her head and jammed her hands on her hips. "To hell with you, Jake Stone. You've tried and convicted me for no reason. I think I lost the comb when I was dancing at the wedding, but I'm not sure. I didn't know how to tell you. I hadn't had a chance to really look for it, and I don't know how Russell got it."

She studied Jake's closed, dark expression. "Do you really think I'd have anything to do with a creep like that? I know you're a suspicious man, Jake, but you're taking this way too far. Don't you realize he's just trying to goad you into a pointless fight? He's probably furious because you've got Rainbow Ranch operating in the black, and now he can't buy it.''

Jake simply glared at her.

''Are you so stupid—or childish—that you can't see what he's trying to do? He knows your weak point, Jake. And so do I. Jealousy.''

His hands clenched into fists, but he didn't move.

''Enough! Go back to the house.''

''Not 'til I've had my say.''

She met his icy gaze straight on. ''Why do you look for ways to find fault with me? You instantly accuse me of flirting with other men if I so much as smile at them.''

''I know what I see.''

''You're so damned blinded by your past, it's amazing you can find the side of the barn.''

She saw him stiffen at the censure and swept on. ''When I went to Sunrise Peaks to see Darryl you asked if I was fishing for a better deal or looking for a lover. I'd already worked a while for you. By then you should've known me better.''

''Finished?''

She met his stony expression without flinching. ''I'm tired of taking the heat for stuff that happened to you years ago. And I'm not going to put up with the way you treat me. You're loving one minute, and crazy jealous the next. What's the matter with you?''

Annie searched his face for any softening, but found none. ''I don't understand this. You know that Ben Russell is a lying snake. But you believe what he says and you don't—or won't—trust me.''

A terrible sense of loss welled up from deep inside. Annie gazed at his cold face, wishing for the warmth of his smile. Her pride took over and she straightened her shoulders.

Quietly she said, ''I love you, Jake. No matter what you want to believe about me. But I can't live with you. Your heart is poisoned. Forever.''

Numb, she went to her bedroom to pack.

Her hand throbbed from her tight grip on the hummingbird comb. God, she didn't want to ever see it again. Her great joy the day Jake gave it to her had turned to her darkest moment when Jake chose to believe Russell's lies.

She left the comb on her dresser and pulled a suitcase out of the closet. She had so little, it was packed in no time.

She lingered, straightening the fragile lace doily on the bureau. A last glance out the window through the white curtains, and she left the room that had been home to her all summer.

Jake waited at the bottom of the stairs, impassive. His eyes blank and hard.

"You're leaving, huh?"

She swallowed and walked down the steps, carrying one bag. At the bottom, she lifted her chin and boldly met his gaze. "Yes. I'll arrange to get the rest of my stuff in the kitchen later."

"You have three days, or it goes out with the other trash."

He thrust a check into her hand. "This includes the final two weeks of the damned contract. Plus a bonus."

"How nice to know you think so highly of me." She gave him a deliberately provocative smile and strolled to the door. Turning, she threw him a kiss. "As Tomás says, *hasta luego.* Until next time."

"There won't be a next time," he growled.

"That's what you think," she muttered, marching to her car. Once inside the shelter of the driver's side, she let her smile fade and started the engine. Her face muscles ached from keeping her artificial smile in place.

Annie drove out of the ranch yard and down Rainbow Road. Her throat was tense, and the roof of her mouth stung from holding back tears. She'd refused to let Jake Stone see her cry.

As if to match her mood, the silver gray strands of a rain shower curtained the valley to the north. There'd be more rainfall at the ranch in an hour, but she wouldn't be around to warm cookies and make coffee or hot chocolate for housebound guests.

"Tough," she told herself. "Let Jake do it."

She wished she could be a fly on the wall, and see what happened when Mr. Macho tried to placate the tenderfeet. Sure, he could live without a lover, but without a cook?

* * *

Annie found a warm welcome at Verna and Buck's.

"So the dang fool lost his temper again?" Buck said, grabbing Annie's suitcase. "He better not make chili for dinner, or the dudes'll stampede."

Verna put an arm around Annie's shoulders. "The foreman's cottage is all set for you. Eat with us?"

"What, break in on you honeymooners? I can fix something for myself."

"Won't hear of it." Verna took a key out of her pocket and unlocked the door to the small house. She led Annie in, coaxing, "Honey, you'll be our first guest. Say yes."

Annie studied her friends' expressions, basking in their warmth and kindness. She choked back tears. "If you'll let me help."

"That's settled," Verna said, shooing Buck out the door. "Lunch'll be ready at noon. Come up to the house. We'll talk."

When the door clicked shut, Annie opened her suitcase.

Her carefully packed straw cowboy hat sat on top, surrounded by a cushion of rolled T-shirts, the crown stuffed with bras and panties. Lifting it from the colorful nest, Annie fingered the brim, remembering the day she'd brought it home to Rainbow. As she'd tried it on, Jake had stood in the doorway and told her she was one very pretty cook. Realizing what could have been between them, she swallowed the lump in her throat.

Sighing, Annie placed the hat on the dresser and turned back to the maplewood bed. Dipping her hand into a side pocket of the case, she brought out a dried rosebud wrapped in white tissue paper, opened it, and sniffed the subtle fragrance. Jake had surprised her with the sweet brier rosebush four days after he'd rescued her from Old Sin, and this had been its first blossom.

Annie's throat constricted. She felt the tight heat of suppressed tears. Hastily, she wrapped the dried rose and tucked it back into the suitcase.

"I won't let him get to me," she declared, unfolding a plaid shirt. Again, memory flooded through her. She'd worn this the day the wild turkey had spooked Sage.

"Jake," she whispered, crushing the shirt against her breasts. Suddenly, her legs wouldn't hold her, and she sat down heavily beside the suitcase. Nuzzling the fabric, she felt the gentle rasp of cotton. They'd made love that day under the tall cottonwoods. She closed her eyes and recaptured the glide of his fingers across her bare skin, the magic of is lips against her mouth, her face, her breasts. A slow, hungry ache swept through her body, and she felt a spasm of grief so intense her stomach churned with nausea. She loved Jake Stone, and he'd thrown her away.

"No!" She jumped to her feet. She wouldn't go easy.

Annie grabbed some jeans and put them away. Jake thought he'd bought her out. That hurt, but she'd already planned to finish her contract to the last day.

She worked in lonely silence, loading socks and underwear into dresser drawers. It would still be hell when she left Rainbow and the man she loved, but at least they'd both know she'd honored their agreement. As she hung the rest of her clothes in the closet, she wondered who was cooking dinner at Rainbow Ranch.

Jake stepped out onto the porch as the Finley family dashed toward him through the heavy rainfall. Annie had only been gone two hours, and already he had to play host. Worse, Finley looked madder than hell, and his two kids were whining like they were going to shrink from a little water.

"Mr. Stone, this weather is intolerable." Finley shook out the spare slicker Annie had kept for guests who ignored the list of suggested clothes. His wife added her litany of complaints as Jake held the door open.

The two brats clamored for something to eat. Hadn't they eaten the lunch Annie'd packed for them? Hastily, he pushed aside all thoughts of her and headed for the kitchen.

Trouble's just starting, Jake thought. Dammit, he was a rancher, not a cook. With this rain, all hell would break loose if he didn't have a hot meal at dinner for the guests. Maybe his chili? He shuddered. Better not. Even he got indigestion from it.

He opened the big refrigerator and found thick steaks in one of Annie's special marinades. He knew how to grill meat. So far, so good. The commercial-size freezer held a motherlode of food: frozen casseroles, stews, cakes, pies, and rolls. On each one, Annie had taped cooking instructions. He pulled out some tidy packages of vegetables, and rustled up dinner.

Afterwards, Jake headed for the stairs and the sanctuary of his room. Let the soggy dudes entertain themselves. He had a bigger problem—Annie. It was obvious she'd planned ahead for the end of her contract at his ranch. It was something he wouldn't expect anyone to do, but she had. She'd always gone the extra mile. "And she's always been honest," he muttered.

Drawn by memories—in spite of all his suspicions—he went into Annie's sitting room. It was neat. Only his grandmother's things were still there. He continued into the bedroom, past a cardboard box with Annie's name on it, and stopped at the mirrored dresser. The smooth wood top was bare, except for the hummingbird comb.

Jake traced the carved bone, then tucked it into his shirt pocket, remembering how pretty it had looked in her red gold hair. "God, I'm a damned fool for even thinking of her."

He caught a flash of green in the mirror and turned toward the open closet. All Annie's clothes were gone except for the dress she'd worn to Prescott the night before. She'd left it behind. "Why?"

He recalled Annie's worn shirts and faded jeans. She'd even mended tears in his clothes and replaced missing buttons. She'd left the dress for another reason. *Because it reminded her of that night, of me?*

He touched the silky fabric, and a hint of Annie's perfume wafted around him.

"Man, you're loco." He jerked his hand away from the dress, and stalked to his room. She was gone for good. He'd get over her Wouldn't he? Or had he just lost his last chance at happiness?

* * *

Morning had come too early. Annie squinted at the illuminated clock face. Four o'clock. She pushed strands of hair away from her eyes and sat up.

Dressed and in her car, she sped toward Rainbow. She had two more weeks of this land that had become home to her. Two more weeks of being near the man she loved in spite of himself.

Rumbling across Gold Creek, she faced the pale darkness in the east. Clouds piled higher, ghostly, menacing. Eerie flashes of distant lightning crackled in their depths. Dawn would come soon, welcomed by all the day critters living on the range. Annie wondered what kind of welcome she'd find.

The kitchen light glowed across the yard when Annie parked in her usual spot. A light shower spattered her as she dashed for the porch. Through the open front door wafted the aroma of fresh coffee. She unzipped her jacket and went toward the source. Jake stood at the sink, facing away from her. Barefoot, he wore jeans but no shirt.

Studying the powerful musculature of his back, divided by the deep groove of his spine, she felt her heartbeat speed up. But she steeled herself for the fight she knew was coming.

Jake pivoted and stood, hands on hips, his eyes as cold and dark as a high mountain lake. "What in blazes are you doing here?"

Annie glared back. "We have a contract. I plan to fulfill it."

"The hell you say. I paid you off yesterday and gave you a hefty bonus to boot."

"I'll work my last two weeks." Annie squared her shoulders. "When I signed our contract, I said you'd lean that I keep my promises. The contract was an agreement between us. I mean to honor that."

Going to the large freezer, she grabbed to pans of cinnamon rolls and put them in the oven. "You told me your word was your bond when you hired me. Damn it, honor that paper we both signed and let me do my job."

"No skin off my nose." He stopped beside the door. "Just stay out of my way."

Annie flinched as the door slammed. She went to work preparing the meal, but her heart ached, and an icy feeling constricted her stomach. Jake obviously hadn't had a change of heart. He probably wanted her out of his life forever.

As the day went on, light showers fell, soaking into the red soil. Most of the guests bowed out of outdoor chores, and Annie added a hearty vegetable-beef soup to the lunch menu.

Late afternoon brought a heavier downpour, and Travis and Jake clomping through the mudroom door.

Dangling his dripping Resistol at arm's length, Travis said, "It's a damned gully-washer out there now." He drowned at the water spattering the kitchen floor. "Sorry for the mess."

"No problem." Annie grabbed a rag and wiped the floor.

Jake jerked his thumb toward the rain beating against the window. "Stay here tonight."

"No way." Annie washed and dried her hands, then went back to forming dinner rolls for the evening meal. "You had Rainbow Road upgraded. I'll be okay."

"Use your brain, for god's sake. Gold Creek is nearly to the top of its banks." Jake's voice was rough, but held a hidden tenderness.

Annie felt the beginning of hope. He did care for her. Why else would he insist she stay?

Jake grabbed her wrist, his strong fingers holding her captive in a careful grip. "Driving back to town is too damned dangerous. I don't want anyone dying on my spread. Stay here."

Annie tugged loose and folded her arms. Her throat ached with suppressed tears. It wasn't her he cared about. Just his ranch's reputation. She took a breath. "I hear you."

He looked at her a moment longer, nodded, and marched out of the kitchen.

Travis scooped up a handful of cookies cooling on the table. "Jake's advice makes sense."

She covered the rolls with a cotton dishtowel and put them aside to rise. "Thanks for caring, Travis. Don't worry. I won't do anything foolish."

As Annie finished the dinner dishes, she watched Jake splash through the rain out to the barn. He'd be there long enough for her to get to her car and leave. No way would she spend the night in the same house with him after what he'd said to her. She grabbed her purse and went into the mudroom for a poncho. Now all she had to do was reach her car.

Annie eased through another stream of muddy water crossing the dirt road as she fought wind-driven rain to keep to the center crown. Her windshield wipers had long since given up the unequal battle against the deluge. She caught quick glimpses of the road ahead in the glare of her high beams, before water rushed to cover the space cleared by the laboring wipers. An eternity seemed to have passed since she'd left the ranch house.

This section of the road dipped down from the low ridge and paralleled Gold Creek. Lightning flared. One long finger licked down, shearing a limb from a cottonwood. Thunder deafened Annie. The thick branch fell across the road, blocking her way.

She stopped a foot from the obstacle and climbed out of the car, bracing herself against the wind and rain that threatened to tear her poncho from her body. A wet blast snatched off her hood. Water plastered her hair to her head and dripped down her neck.

Above the fury of the storm, she heard the roar of Gold Creek. It raced past her, dark muddy waters tearing at the rocky bank. A tree at the edge trembled, tipped into the water, and tumbled away, taking a section of the red earth.

Fighting the power of the wind, Annie opened her door and climbed back into the car. She closed her eyes for a moment, grateful for the shelter. Water had seeped under her poncho. She shivered in wet jeans and shirt. Even her bra and panties were damp.

It couldn't be helped. She started the engine and worked around the edge of the leafy barrier until she got back on to the road.

Once past the grove of trees, she braked at the sight revealed by another burst of lightning. The bridge, its white paint peeled and weathered, stood like a white ghost in the path of tumbling, frothing red water. Sticks, small branches, and other debris rode the crest, diving under the wooden bridge, brushing the bottom. While Annie watched, a tree crashed against the railing. Its roots and branches tangled in the vertical poles.

Crossing the bridge was too dangerous. As much as she hated to admit it, she had to go back to Jake's house. Rain made it impossible to see through her rear window. Annie shoved open the door and stepped out into the violent storm. A low rumble came from the racing creek. Probably rocks knocked loose by the flood, and swept downstream.

Her skin tingled. Her hair lifted. *Lightning!* She dove into the protection of the car barely ahead of the blinding flash and blast of thunder. Sparks danced and sizzled along the skin of the hood. Annie tucked her hands away from metal and smelled a peculiar sharp tang in the air. Behind her, twin trees exploded and fell across the road, cutting off any retreat.

Now she had no choice but to go ahead before the rising water reached the car with her inside, and swept it into the swift creek.

As Annie drove onto the bridge, it shuddered and groaned under the battering of water, rocks, and trees. Ahead, a geyser erupted from a widening crack in the bridge roadbed. Slamming the car into reverse, Annie prayed as it lurched backward. Her rear wheels spun on the slick clay. The car slid to one side, and stopped at the creek edge. Then the engine coughed and died.

"No!" She turned the key in the ignition. Muddy water surrounded the car, rising with a speed that stunned her. The car rocked. Water crept under the doors, and Annie knew she had to get out before the sedan floated into the river.

She wrenched the handle and kicked at the door. Through the opening, water poured in, shocking her with its icy fingers.

Struggling to climb out, she fought the relentless force of the flood. Something hidden in the murk struck her ankle. Her feet slid out from under her.

She lost her grip on the frame and cried, "Jake," as muddy water closed over her head.

Chapter Sixteen

Jake stood at the study window, one hand braced on the frame. Lightning flared against the night. Raindrops gathered in pools illuminated by the yard light. Thank God Annie wasn't driving in that wild rain and wind.

Something nagged at him. He rubbed the back of his neck. He hadn't seen her since he'd gone to the barn after dinner to check on one of the mares.

"Damn, where's her car?" He noticed her empty parking spot, then searched beyond the other cars and trucks.

"Gone!"

He breathed a curse. Annie was driving to town in this hellish storm.

He grabbed the phone, punched in the number, and waited, fear clawing at his gut.

Verna answered on the fourth ring. "Annie? You okay?"

His throat tightened. "She isn't there yet?" Another stroke of lightning lit water sheeting across the window.

"No! Me and Buck was on the porch watchin' for her." The growl of thunder punctuated Verna's words.

"Dammit, Jake, why'd you let Annie leave? She should've stayed at the ranch tonight. You jackass. Ever since Annie started workin' at Rainbow, she's knocked herself out for you. What did she get in return? Suspicion and a load of bull."

"She—"

"Now she's out there drivin', and this's worse than the night Steph—"

"The night Stephanie died," Jake said grimly. "I know." Muffled voices beyond the closed door reminded him of other people in the house. "I'll go look for Annie."

"Find her, Jake." Verna's voice softened. "And you be careful."

He dropped the handset into its cradle, and went through the kitchen door, already making plans.

"Coffee, boss?" Nick held up the pot.

"I'm goin' after Annie." Jake headed for his rain slicker and hat in the mudroom.

The lanky young man followed, and stood in the doorway. "She's driving to Verna's? Even after you warned her?"

Jake nodded, closing the snaps on his bright yellow raincoat. "Travis left before dark on a family emergency. He won't be back tonight. Steve and Tomás are on the high range. They'll stay at the line cabin until morning. You'll have to ride herd on the guests."

Finley marched into the kitchen. "Mr. Stone, this is insufferable. The power keeps going out."

"Lines are down. Nick started the generator."

"I should hope so. We paid good money for our stay." He frowned at Jake. "You're leaving? What if there's an emergency?"

"Nick'll be here."

"This kid?" Finley made a dismissive gesture. "Where are the men?"

"This is a working ranch, mister, and right now one of my people is in trouble. You and your family sit tight."

Jake grabbed his hat and flashlight. "You're in charge, Nick. Any trouble, Clint will back you up." He fixed the dude with a level stare. "Clint's a retired Green Beret."

Jake left the man spluttering and stepped out into the storm. Wind slammed into him and ripped at his slicker. The path to the corral had become a muddy stream.

Once inside the barn, he saddled Bandit, mentally mapping all the low spots and rockslide areas on the ranch road. With his lariat secured to the saddle, Jake rode out into the howling night.

The stallion snorted at the lashing wind and rain. Jake rubbed his prize horse's neck, fighting to keep his own frantic concern for Annie under control. "C'mon, boy. You're Annie's best chance."

He kneed his mount into an easy lope, lighting the way with his powerful flashlight. They swept down the hill, past where he'd first kissed Annie. He slammed the door on that memory.

Why the hell had she put herself in danger tonight? He knew why, dammit. He hadn't apologized. He'd barely talked to her. Just treated her like hired help, to save his foolish pride. He should've stayed with Annie in the house after dinner, made sure she didn't leave.

Guiding Bandit toward a dip in the road he muttered, "How much longer?" The stallion shied at a heavier burst of wind-driven rain, then lunged through the fast-flowing water to the other side.

The weather had been like this the night he looked for Stephanie. He'd been frantic with worry. This time it was even worse. This time the woman he truly loved could die because he'd been stupid.

Jake dismounted, examined the higher patch of ground, and found part of a tire track. Annie had made it this far. Had she reached safety, or was she in danger?

When he finally topped the Gold Creek overlook, Jake swore at the sight of the flood swirling above creek banks. The broken bridge rails showed ghostly white. Water raced across the roadbed, and Jake felt his stomach freeze at the mental picture of Annie on the bridge.

As he headed Bandit down the rain-slicked road, they crossed the debris line. If Annie'd been trapped—

He cut off the thought. She had to be safe! He loved her. If only he'd buried his foolish doubts and told her.

Picking their way through fallen cottonwood branches, Jake searched for signs of Annie. The black stallion's hooves splattered mud. He laid his ears back against the discomfort of rain, and threaded a path between lightning-scorched tree trunks.

A flash of lightning revealed Annie's car nose-down in the

creek, caught in a tangle of fallen trees and parts of the bridge. Jake choked back a curse, haunted by the ghastly memory of Stephanie's lifeless body crumpled in a jumble of branches and mud.

Another flare of light showed the passenger section above water, but the whole car shuddered with blows from chunks of debris.

He stood in his stirrups and shouted, "Annie!" into the wild night. Was she alive?

Propelled by fear, he stripped off hat, boots, and slicker, tied one end of his rope to the pommel, the other under his arms, and plunged into the deadly current.

He fought to reach the passenger side of the car where the door was above water.

Annie hugged the thick branch of a fallen sycamore. Water dragged at her feet and ankles as she clung to the precarious perch, stranded in the center of a wild flood. Through the thick wood, she felt the vibration of current-driven debris hitting her refuge. The metallic screech of wood and rocks battering her drowned car set her teeth on edge. How could she cross the swift current racing past on both sides? She had to before she was swept away when the tree broke loose from its sandstone anchor.

Huddled in her poncho, and deafened by rain and thunder, she hadn't known Jake was on the bank until she saw him tie a rope to Bandit's saddle and plunge into Gold Creek.

"Jake," she cried, but the wind tore the words from her mouth and smothered them in the storm's fury.

Another bolt lit the scene. Bandit stood, four legs set, as Jake swam in powerful strokes toward her unstable island. He stopped behind the car, out of sight.

She screamed his name, over and over, hoping he'd move to the front of the car and see her clinging to the wood. Her heart hammered in her chest as she watched him come into view at the passenger window. He peered inside, then moved parallel to the buried engine and looked in the direction of the uprooted tree where she clung. He waved as his lips formed her name.

He saw her!

She wanted to weep with relief. Jake was coming to her, propelling himself along the sedan and around the deep sandstone trap. He'd rescue her. He'd—

As if in slow motion, a thick log loomed up, gave Jake a glancing blow to the head, then tumbled away into the dark. His hand slipped off the car. Only the rope kept him from following the log.

Frozen in fear, she saw his head loll forward, jerk up, and wobble. A heavier burst of rain veiled his lonely struggle.

She couldn't let him die.

Annie scrambled down the rough bark, fighting to keep him in sight. The plastic poncho snagged in a broken-off branch, choking her. No time to waste. Blindly, she tore free and spun away into the savage flood. She gasped at the shocking cold, coughed on a mouthful of thick, muddy water, and spat it out; but her whole being strained toward Jake.

Praying, she kicked and dog-paddled upstream, and suddenly his head appeared.

Her right hand brushed a taut rope and she seized it. She clung to the line stretched between him and Bandit, as stiff fibers in the rope scraped across her palms and fingers.

Treacherous currents flung her against a boulder, its top a scant foot above water. Trapped between it and the rope, she saw Jake, a darker shadow ahead of her in the flood, grab the car's rear bumper.

Clinging to cracks in the weathered granite, she shouted his name into the wind. He plunged toward her, breasting the heavy flow as Bandit, true to his training, maneuvered to keep the rope taut. When Jake came close enough, she grabbed his sleeve. Fighting the raw force of the water, they labored together until he lodged against the boulder.

Exhausted and shivering, she leaned her cheek on the cold stone. How could she go any farther, do anymore? Jake wrapped one arm around her. His body protected her head and back from the ferocious pressure of the flood, but underwater currents still battered her legs.

"We'll make it," Jake shouted. Rope scraped along Annie's

side and she gasped. Jake's hold tightened on her and the great
stallion slowly backed away from the edge, drawing his human
burden through the raging creek.

Annie's head went under. She held her breath and fought
back to the surface. Jake's grasp loosened, then grew more
secure. Time lost its meaning as they battled to keep from
drowning in the deadly onrush of water.

More jagged timbers broke away from the bridge and a
splintered trestle blocked their path. Jake pushed Annie around
the end, grasped the rope, and yanked. Nothing happened.
Annie realized the line had tangled in ragged wood.

She fought a surge of hopelessness. Bandit had kept the rope
taut. Now, when she and Jake needed the Stallion's greater
strength to pull them to the bank, the horse couldn't help.

Jake curled her fingers around a thick rail, and set his mouth
to her ear. "Hang on," he said, then disappeared beneath the
muddy flow.

In numbed horror, she watched the place where he'd gone
under. Below water, his body brushed hers, then his head broke
the surface beside her.

He gulped in a deep breath and ducked under again. She
slammed one hand against the surface in an agony of fear.
"Dammit, Jake. I'll kill you if you drown."

After endless moments, he popped to the surface, and she
wanted to cover him with kisses.

"Got it." He braced one hand on the thick timber as he
coughed and pawed water off his face.

"J-J-Jake." She couldn't make her teeth stop chattering.

He touched her cheek. "C'mon." His arm slipped around
her, but her numbed fingers wouldn't release their hold on the
wood. She pried at them with her other trembling hand, biting
her lip at the pain. Locked muscles refused to budge.

"Now, Annie!" Jake had placed his body between her and
the main current. She heard him grunt as he deflected another
chunk of heavy debris.

More adrenaline raced through her bloodstream, and she
painfully jerked her hand away, but her fingers stayed rigidly
curved.

Then, with Jake's arm securely around her, and Bandit once
more exerting a steady pull, they held their heads above water
and made for shore.

Annie's knee struck something hard. Jake tugged on her,
shouting for her to stand. She pushed to her hands and knees.
He helped her up. Clinging to each other, they staggered out
of the flood's grip, then sprawled in the mud.

Jake's arm fell away from Annie. He groaned and rolled
onto his back.

Alarmed, she knelt beside him. He lay panting, the rope still
around his upper chest as Bandit held the tension. Jake tried
to sit, but the stallion set his hooves and pulled. Jake fell
backward with a moan.

The thunder and lightning had moved in the direction of town,
but rain pelted harder under a driving wind. Annie huddled over
the man she loved, trying to protect him from the storm. She
knew even his great strength had been sapped by fighting the
flood.

His legs shifted fitfully. He mumbled, "Bandit. Rope."
Groaning, he plucked at the lasso biting into his flesh.

"What can I do?" she cried, feeling totally helpless, and
certain Jake would die of exposure if she didn't get him loose.
She looked up at Bandit, a dark, fearfully strong beast, and
whimpered.

A shudder wracked Jake's body, and the stallion hauled the
rope even tighter. Annie saw Jake go rigid with pain.

"No!" She shot to her feet.

As she walked toward the great quarter horse, a small voice
whispered in her head, "Don't show fear."

Don't show fear? Her knees quaked. Her breath came short
and hard. Holding her wet, wind-whipped hair out of her eyes,
she forced herself to breathe deeply. She recalled Jake's quiet
voice as he calmed a restless horse, and began crooning, "Nice
Bandit. Good horse. I'm your friend. Don't be afraid." *Who
am I kidding? I'm the one who's scared.*

In the glare of a single lightning bolt she saw Bandit's eyes
roll. He held his head low, tucked in at the nose with his ears

laid back. Suddenly all the horror stories of horses in a rage froze her into terrified immobility.

Jake needs me. In a strangely disembodied state, she rested a hand on Bandit's shoulder. "Easy, boy," she soothed, while inside she screamed, *Jake's hurting.*

The horse snuffled at her neck. She stood her ground, her pulse roaring in her ears. Rain and wind buffeted her. Bandit explored her hair, warming the side of her face with his breath.

"C'mon, boy," she whispered, and collected his reins. The leather stung her raw skin and she bit her lip, but she tugged him toward Jake. The quarter horse snorted and followed Annie like a pet dog.

They reached the stricken man. Working by touch and the pale glow of distant lightning reflected off clouds, Annie loosened the water-soaked knot in the rope and slid it over Jake's head.

He rolled to his hands and knees, paused, dragging in deep breaths, then turned and sat up. Bandit lowered his muzzle to sniff Jake's hair and back.

Annie crouched beside them, vaguely aware that the rain had stopped. She placed her hand on Jake's shoulder. "Can you stand?"

"Give me a few minutes." He raised his face as if testing the air. "We're gonna be all right. Even the wind's dying down."

Bandit nudged his master.

Annie plopped down beside Jake and hugged her knees, trying to get warm. He wrapped one arm around her, and with a gentle finger turned her face toward him. "God, Annie," he took her into his embrace. "I thought I'd never again see you alive."

She trembled in his arms, too filled with tears and joy to speak.

He rubbed her shoulder. "Got to get you home, warm you up." He struggled to his feet, swaying. Annie slipped an arm around him while he steadied.

Turning her into his embrace once more, he held her close. "You scared the hell out of me."

Annie shivered as she recalled the log hitting him and his desperate efforts to free himself from the tightening rope. "Look who's talking."

Jake located his slicker and draped it around Annie, worried by her chilled skin. With hands made clumsy from the cold, he grabbed his hat, boots, and flashlight.

"Annie, we'd better huddle together under the slicker. Share our body heat."

"Oh, boy. Two drowned rats on horseback." She gave him the raincoat with a flash of her old spirit. "No fooling around this time."

He started to lift her into the saddle, but she pulled away. "Don't you dare, after the way Bandit jerked you around." She scrambled up, settled in, and gave him an encouraging smile. "See, as Buck says, you larned me good."

Setting his jaw against aching bones and muscles, he swung up behind her and tucked her into his protective hold. Annie leaned against him, her head sheltered by his hat, and held the waterproof garment closed. He felt shudders wracking her slim frame, and tightened his grip. "We're heading home to a warm bath," he kissed the side of her neck, "and bed."

"No argument from me."

Relieved by her quick acceptance, Jake switched on the flashlight and guided Bandit through a wild mix of splintered wood and branches. They passed the crest above Gold Creek, and Bandit chose a careful trail along Rainbow Road.

Jake rested his chin on the top of Annie's head, achingly aware of how close she'd come to death. Now, before he lost his courage, he had to tell her what was in his heart. Her answer would sentence him to happiness or an empty life.

Annie slipped one hand out from beneath the slicker and rested it on his cheek. "Jake, you probably don't want to hear this again, but I love you."

Stunned, he couldn't answer. He could barely absorb the fact that she really did love him.

His silence must have seemed like a rejection to her. She tucked her hand back under the coat and sighed.

He guided Bandit around a washed-out place in the road, and cleared his throat, not knowing where to begin. "Annie, I fell in love with you the day I saw you in my house. Like you belonged there. With me. I was just too bullheaded to admit it to myself. And you're right about Ben Russell. He knows just how to make me crazy angry. I didn't know what I was doin' or sayin' when he waved that little comb at me."

"Oh, Jake—"

"Wait, honey, let me finish." He kissed the top of her head, wondering how much longer he had to hold her, kiss her, make love to her. "Do you love me enough to get married and stay on Rainbow cookin' for dudes? Or do you want to take the job for Regency? Be a world-famous chef?"

Annie shivered, and he rubbed her arm. He wanted to kiss her until she surrendered, until she promised to stay forever, but she had to choose.

"Jake, look." She pointed to the sky.

With the rainstorm past, clouds scudded away in the wind across midnight blue mountains. The moon floated high, surrounded by a luminous circular rainbow. The wet road to the ranch glistened and two coyotes sang a duet in the distance.

Minutes passed. Annie didn't say another word. Jake knew he'd lost her.

Waiting in silence, he took a deep, anxious breath, and bit back a moan. Hell, his ribs ached, his head throbbed, even his callused hands were rubbed raw. Every rocking movement in the saddle hurt, and he welcomed the pain. He deserved it for the pain he'd caused Annie, the humiliation he'd heaped on her.

He'd driven her away because of stupid suspicions. And, God help him, he'd been cruel. He inwardly cursed his idiotic behavior, and the stubbornness that had destroyed his dream of home and family.

Annie stirred in his arms. "Jake, I've never been so cold or so happy in my life." She reached back and pressed her hand against his cheek. "Yes, I'll marry you. And I'll never leave you. I swear it on that rainbow."

He turned her against his chest, and fastened his lips on hers. With a soft cry, she clung to him.

Deep in his heart the cold places dissolved. He wrapped her closer in his embrace and knew they were truly going home together.

About the Author

Jean Clark was born in California and has explored many of the beaches, mountains, canyons, and deserts of the Southwest. When she's not writing or reading, she quilts or gardens.

She lives in Southern California, where she volunteers at the Orange County Chapter of Romance Writers of America.

You can write to her at:

P.O. Box 173

Cypress, CA 90630